T0113595

69 JERUSALEM STREET

and other stories

69 JERUSALEM STREET
and other stories

Lindiwe Nkutha

Publication © Modjaji Books 2020
Text © Lindiwe Nkutha 2020
First published in 2020 by Modjaji Books Pty Ltd
www.modjajibooks.co.za

ISBN 978-1-928433-04-0 (Print)
ISBN 978-1-928433-03-3 (ePub)

Edited by Katlego Tapala
Cover artwork and lettering by Jesse Breytenbach
Author photograph by Rorisang Putu
Book design and layout by Liz Gowans

Set in Aldine401 BT

NATIONAL INSTITUTE
FOR THE HUMANITIES
AND SOCIAL SCIENCES

This work is based on the research supported by the National Institute
for the Humanities and Social Sciences

*This book is dedicated to all the women who, in their own way,
have shaped the person I am and am becoming.
Especially those from whom I come:
uNaRadebe, uMaMfusi, and uMaMgoza.*

CONTENTS

Rock   9

69 Jerusalem Street   25

The Glasspecker   39

Confessions of Karelina   52

The Reader   63

Black Widow   79

Jocasta's Hairballs   95

JV Mdluli Estates   128

Rock

Now, as far as music goes, I've always preferred rock 'n' roll and nothing else. I love the kind of guitar sound that fills my head and pulls my heart in different directions. In fact, I've always dreamt of learning to play the guitar one day. Just like my mother, even though she hasn't played in a long time. I guess this is how the nickname 'Rock' stuck to me. What I should really say is, I hope that is how. The truth is different though, and it wears many faces. One version, which I suspect is truer than most, has a little something to do with the fact that I've been rocking and rolling – on my makeshift wheelchair, that is – since I was seven. Throughout my childhood, I had to make peace with the other children in my neighbourhood whispering 'rock 'n' roll' every time I rocked and wheeled myself from my house to the shops, and from school to my house.

I lost both my legs to hunger. Thanks to the ravenous appetite of our neighbour's dog which had not been fed for over a week, my legs were mistaken for lamb shanks. As a teenager, I managed to convince myself that it was no intentional ill will on the dog's part, just a hunger that could not be ignored. I could relate to that. There were moments in my life when I, too, had been so hungry I fantasised about eating the same dog. I guess the dog got to what was on both our minds before I did, and I thought that was fair. This thought reminded me of a bumper sticker pasted on the back of a guitar that stood next to my mother's bed, the same one she had not played in years: EAT OR BE EATEN, it said.

My mother, who was as inconsistent as she was pragmatic, did not share this philosophical analysis of my fate. She was determined to sue our neighbours for my deformation, in the same way she had seen people do on American television. Had it not been for Malum' Justice's intervention she may have actually gone ahead and done just that.

It was Malum' Justice, my mother's younger brother – and the only member of my family to have spent more than two semesters at a university in his short-lived attempt to study the law – who pointed out to his sister that in order to sue, one had to have some money in the first place.

'To pay the lawyers, Sis' Ncedi,' he had said in a voice befitting a freshly- struck-off-the-roll barrister, in answer to the 'Why?' that never quite made it from my mother's lips.

It was a fact that did not need stating that Sis' Ncedi did not have any determinable coins to rub together. In fact, there were church mice that had managed a level of affluence higher than hers, both by human and mouse standards.

There are a lot of things that I find do not make a lot of cents – I mean sense – in my head. The list, if I cared enough to produce one, would stretch to the horizon. So, every now and then, I allow different puzzles to drift in and out of my mind. Just last week, I wondered about two things. The first was why it is that people with money find it necessary to rub coins against each other. The second was why Mother, who as I have already said was a woman who did not have any coins to call her own, let alone rub together, had wanted to sue people who had even less than she?

Bra Phandi's dog was the culprit.

Bra Phandi was the sort of fellow who fits neatly into the government's newspeak-inspired definition of 'previously and currently disadvantaged'. A feat which life accomplished for him when the Unharmonious Gold Mines closed down and lost him his job. Exactly six years before his dog mistook me for Sunday lunch.

Sis' Ntokozo, Bra Phandi's wife and sole breadwinner for that same period, had over the years developed a case of arthritis so severe, the only comfortable position she could find for her hands was suspending them in the air. This habit gave her the aura of a piano maestro at strain to decide which concerto to play next. So acute was her condition that the flood of laundry which had once flowed into her house demanding that she wade through it for pay – if pay is what it could be called – soon dried up and made her and Bra Phandi first runners up in the privation contest.

All of that changed, though, when Bra Phandi, realising that their condition was not about to alter itself anytime soon, decided to make peace with the hand that life had dealt him. To his credit, he took over his wife's duties and established himself as the neighbourhood's first male washerwoman – a move which earned him instant brownie points with all the women folk and again opened up the floodgates of laundry.

When he decided to be entrepreneurial about his new vocation suggestive grunts referring to him as 'Aunty Phandi' soon vanished to the communal gut of swallowed words. The first thing that showed that he meant business, was the improvised billboard, followed by the ubiquitous pamphlets bearing his name and the services he offered. These were handed out house-to-house and at every street corner by his overly zealous army of sales representatives

– neighbourhood children aching to supplement their non-existent weekly allowances. He paid 50 cents for every distributed pamphlet that resulted in actual business. In no time, our whole area was awash with 'BRA PHANDI WASHERWOMAN ENTERPRISES'. In one stroke, Bra Phandi had managed to turn the mundane chore of washing other people's clothes into a lucrative business and news over which countless cups of tea were drunk.

'At least he is being responsible and manly enough to take care of his wife. Something we can't say about the lot of you,' Green Mamba used to say.

Green Mamba was a woman who lived two streets away from us, a friend of no one in particular. She ordinarily went by the name Jacqoubeth, when she was not being spoken of by my uncle.

Malum' Justice would say, 'There is nothing that anyone who walks around wearing a green towel so skunky and worn that it brings up images of a snake shedding, deserves to be called other than "Green Mamba."'

He presented a really persuasive case. So, in my mind too, Jacqoubeth began to exist as Green Mamba.

'At least she is nothing like your work-shy-beer-thirsty stingy backside, linked to a head full of a tiny knowledge of the law, Justice!' my mother said as rejoinder in support of the green one every time Malum' Justice expressed a different opinion.

He had made it his business to always do that. He called it 'the art of being contrary'. In his larynx he carried a barrage of retorts, of which he had perfected the flair of administering. Not a word was lost with him. He was so particular about his words that he would not utter a single one unless he knew that its departure from his lips was destined for a bullseye: where it hurt the most. Where he felt defeated by my mother – and this was seldom – he always resorted to asking her the one question he knew she wasn't willing to entertain.

'Awusho, Ncedi, do you ever intend on restringing that guitar that has been showing us its armadillo smile for what is beginning to now feel like eternity?'

He knew that if there was a line guaranteed to silence my mother and sully her mood, that was the one.

Although the grin of the toothless guitar, nobly resting on a small strip of red carpet, was one we woke up to every morning, like me, no one spoke about it. It stood leaning against our wooden kitchen scheme, which was itself precariously held together by fewer than three nails and kept erect by what remained in the wood's cellular memory of when it used to be a tree. No one who knew what was good for them dared bring up the subject of the guitar or its original owner.

There was a loud but unspoken pact between my mother's friends and customers to keep silent about the guitar. In order to achieve the near impossible double exploit of keeping her mind off the guitar while earning a living my mother had started operating a casino out of the capsule we called home. I guess 'casino' is an elaborate but suitable term to describe a place where women and men congregated with the sole purpose of winning, but most likely losing, a little money.

They came. All sorts. They came to make sacrifices to gods with unknown names. But, for their sorrows and joys alike they offered libations to each other under the pretext of offering these to their gods. Yoked to each other, they massed to help lug the crosses lassoed around their necks, the weight of which seemed to them lighter when carried as a shared burden.

I used to watch them from the vantage point of my Rockmobile. I would study their faces and tell myself stories about them. That was the only way I got to know them. None of them ever spoke to me. To them I was in every sense as good as everything Ncedi owned: there but not fully functional and thus not worthy of any serious attention.

In our capsule, mind travel rapidly became my favourite pastime and the most entertaining reprieve from the punishing disregard I felt from others. Seeing as it was difficult for me to physically move myself from one place to another, I resolved very early on that I would not keep my thoughts imprisoned in this body that seldom went further than the distance to school.

My favourite destination had become any place where I could sneak a peek at human interaction outside my own home. From time to time my imagination transported me from the faces of my mother's co-gamblers to their homes, where I could create fantasies about what they had or had not eaten for breakfast. I would imagine whom they had woken up next to that morning. I would imagine whom it was they went home to account to, on those days when they lost at cards. But also, I would imagine on whose faces the smiles would land, on the very rare occasion that they won. As a result, people's faces had a way of engraving themselves on my mind, and I became one of those people who could confidently state without fear of being proven wrong that I never forgot a face. That is how I came to know all my mother's regulars.

One of my favourite faces was a man I had secretly christened 'The Glove'. In my world, real names did not have much currency. I figured that, since no one knew mine, there was little point in me knowing anyone else's, except for those that circumstance demanded I know. The Glove, to me, looked like a decrepit glove which had once belonged to a boxer who had never won a match in his life. He had what the kids in our neighbourhood called 'skhumba touch' – a variation of scurvy that did not only attach itself to his skin but to his personality and clothes as well.

My gift for remembering faces was useful for the purpose of spotting newcomers, a service which I offered my mother for free. It was important for her because she used it to hustle those whose defences had not yet been solidly built up. We also kept a close eye on anyone new, treating them with lavish suspicion until they proved themselves differently. This is why, on that Thursday, I could not release my gaze from the bizarre picture that gradually took shape right in front of my eyes. Even in my transfixed state, a lingering feeling told me that I had seen this apparition before. Perhaps not in this life but seen it I had.

It was wearing a purple hat with two quail feathers on either side and a brown corduroy jacket that looked like it had not been washed since 1994. As I looked on, the figure changed from resembling a man to resembling a woman with such speed I could not keep up. My mind set about in a frantic hunt for clues and started with the most apparent offender: the corduroy jacket. From where I was sitting it looked very masculine but with a distinctly feminine feel about it. Perhaps the shoulder pads. But then again, poor people never make much of a fuss over the gender of their clothing.

The figure's bottom half was clad in a slick pair of pants, the type I suspect would have been just the thing to be seen in on the streets of Sophiatown. The shoes were the obligatory brown and white two-toned kind – the kind a pair of pants like that clearly wanted to rest its turn-ups on. They appeared two sizes smaller than a regular man's shoes and they were also the only part of the apparel that was still intact. To complete the picture, there hung on its face a pair of goggles that looked as if they had sprung straight out of a 1960s clothing catalogue.

After a lot of mental struggle I decided that it was a man, based solely on how he walked: a swanky, rhythmic right-heel-forward-right-shoulder-back; a shuffle-like drag of the left foot forward and a jive-like twist of the left shoulder forward. I decided to hold on to this conviction until my mind and I had gathered evidence to the contrary.

As he advanced, I saw that he held a bouquet of yellow roses, which would have been adorable had he not smothered them to death on his way over. Or maybe they were already dead when he got them.

He surprised me by walking straight towards me. He surprised me even more when he squatted next to my Rockmobile and opened his mouth to speak. To me! Apart from my mother and Malum' Justice, no one had spoken to me in six years. It was confirmed to me at that point that he was a newcomer. It was only they that made the mistake of actually speaking to me.

I lie. There was also the praying mantis that had taken residence within the twigs of our straw broom. Although, technically speaking, insects don't count as people, she spoke to me. If truth be told – for truth always demands permission before it is told – maybe the mantis spoke more about me than to me. She would clasp her hands, focus her gaze on the sky and speak to someone she referred to as Gold. She would have these long conversations with this person, Gold, who to me seemed to live in some place beyond the clouds. It was in the way that the mantis spoke that I developed this theory. There was something in the mantis's voice that suggested, despite her skyward facing posture, that it was really a place beyond the sky that she wanted her words to reach. I concluded that this was where this Gold person must live.

They were mostly about me, these conversations.

For instance, the mantis would say 'Ohhhh Gold, please guarantee this child a golden future,' or 'Ohhhh Gold, if only you would help her walk again!'

I came to believe that this Gold person was either hard of hearing or just didn't care. Hard of hearing, because everyone I had heard speaking to him, including my mother on occasion that she did, found it necessary to do so at the top of their voice. Gold did not care because he never responded to any of the requests that either she or the mantis placed before him. Personally, I thought it would make much more sense if Goldie relocated from that place on the other side of the sky to some place more practical like, say, the Carlton Centre. Although we would still have to pay to speak to him, as we did in church, at least this time he would be much closer and better able to hear. And then, perhaps those who spoke to him would give up the need to shout when they addressed him.

All the same, I found the mantis a good companion and an unobtrusive babysitter. The best of its kind, with minimum demands: no payment, no unemployment insurance, just boarding and lodging. At this thought, I wondered about something else. I wondered how many mantises lived in the northern suburbs of Johannesburg, subsisting on prayer, boarding and lodging. My mind then hopped to Mevrou Zootvlei – Sis' Ntokozo's madam before she became our maestro.

Mevrou Zootvlei – I am not even sure if that was her real name. 'OohMmedem', is what Sis' Ntokozo called her.

'Ag tog, but she was sweet. Just never paid attention to detail. Never paid anyone anything, really.' I remember her once saying, a couple of months after Sis' Ntokozo fell sick, 'Ag, Nothokozo, man. According to me, I think it would be much easier and cheaper, man, for julle almal if you came and lived by me.'

The funny thing is that in the eight years we had lived next door to Bra Phandi and Sis' Ntokozo, I had come to believe that the woman's name was Ntokozo. But white people are funny that way. They never hesitate to call you whatever their tongues can muster.

I was in the middle of imagining what my name would sound like rolling off a white person's tongue if they cared enough to say it. In my head I was playing around with and fumbling for variations of the pronunciation of my name, each time, trying for things that sounded a bit but not quite like my real name – Zimbabushiso, perhaps? My train of thought was interrupted by the sound of the apparition's voice.

'Zibusiso,' he said, in a voice that sounded distinctly like a woman's. 'So, this is where you and Ncedi have been hiding all these years. Is she here?'

Caught for a moment by the shock, I couldn't answer – my silence possibly a confirmation for him that physically disabled people are also mentally challenged. He spoke again, this time slowly.

Only, at this point, I was beginning to change my mind about him. He was increasingly becoming – in both demeanour and decorum – a woman. My mind and I almost agreed that he was a she.

'Zibusiso, is your mother home?'

I had to quickly swallow the Zambezi River of saliva jamming my throat before I responded.

'She's not back from church yet, but she should be back any moment now,' I said, trying to suppress the quiver in my voice.

'Is it okay if I wait in here for a while, until she comes back?' she asked.

Her tender voice and soft eyes, which I had stolen a glance at the second she took off her goggles, brought my mind and me to total agreement. She was a she.

I nodded in response to her question. She grabbed an empty crate of beer that stood next to the guitar and then froze for a moment, as if she and the guitar were being reacquainted. I could swear, although at this point I was certain of precious little, that the guitar actually nodded to acknowledge her presence.

Zibusiso! She knew my name! Oh, how I so wanted to ask her how she knew my name! No one knew my name. I was 'Ncedi's daughter', someone whose name was never uttered.

'I see she kept the guitar,' she said, half speaking to me, half muttering to herself.

'We've had it for a very long time,' I said, even though I was not sure she wanted an answer. 'One day, when I start my rock 'n' roll band, I will play it,' I said, when my mother walked in.

'Now, child, who are you talking to?'

My mother had barely finished asking when the answer to that question sprang nervously from the beer crate it was sitting on.

'Ncedi!' it said.

'Dan! Danisile, is that you?!' My mother walked up to the answer and gave it a hug.

For a moment, it felt as if time's pattern was disrupted. In each other's embrace, the past kissed the future and the present didn't seem to mind. That was one version of the truth. The kind I preferred. One which I also inferred circumstance had forced Ncedi and Danisile to ignore.

'Shooo, Dan!' my mother said repeatedly, sounding like someone trying to dislodge herself from a trance. Her jaw shook hands with her neck and a river of tears welled up in her eyes.

'I thought they said …' my mother began.

'Yes, I know, but I'm not,' Dan interrupted her.

'But they said … They said they had papers to prove it,' Ncedi continued.

'They said a lot of things, I know. But, as you can see, I am not. It wasn't true. Just like the many things they said about you,' Dan said, extending her arm to give my mother the wilted roses.

Right there in the middle of the casino, with all her sympathisers looking on, my mother's well of joy stole its first drop from a passing cloud. My mother and Dan stood looking at each other, oblivious of time and everyone else in the room. They continued their conversation, which from the looks of it did not need a great quantity of words to keep it moving.

As an observer, I was not too sure what they were talking about but they knew, and somehow, that was enough. The smile I saw on my mother's face was also reassurance that whatever was being shared was good news. She wore a hearty smile, a kind I had not seen on her since I lost my legs.

Despite most of the conversation being lost on me, there were at least three graspable things I thought I heard said.

The first was by my mother when she said to Dan, 'Come sit outside, it's quieter there. You have so much to tell me.'

The second was Dan's jack-in-the-just-opened-box question, 'Do you still play?'

There was no verbal response to this question. Perhaps, feeling ashamed, my mother had nodded yes, or honestly shook her head for a no. I will never know. My mother is the one always telling me not to enter the business of old people, so, for a spell, I was satisfied with hearing just what I heard.

The next thing I heard was said three minutes before a Soweto sunset, when those who owned TV sets prepared themselves for a daily dose of 'Days of Our Lives', and those who didn't, contemplated theirs.

They spoke for a while afterwards, things that my ears were too lazy to catch.

'You haven't done too badly for yourself, Ncedi,' Dan said, as she got up, readying to say her goodbyes.

'Not exactly what I dreamt of but at least I have a place to call home,' was my mother's part abashed, part proud response.

A moment passed without a word from either of them. In that moment, in search of activity to keep my mind occupied, I caught a glimpse of the most orange sun setting. I heard the sands hissing their way through countless hourglasses on the horizon. I spied on the praying mantis peeping from under the broom in a way I had seen Sis' Ntokozo do on days when she felt too embarrassed to ask for a cup of mealie meal. I saw a green fly dallying over the decision to end its journey. It finally decided on Danisile's lip as its target, more as an act of conspiring to give her an excuse to say something than as preference. When the fly landed on Dan's lip, she and my mother both laughed, breaking their silence.

'I see you kept it,' Dan said, using her head to gesture at the guitar.

This time she was not muttering.

My mother gave an audible response, sparing my now curious neck from straining in my attempt to enter old people's news.

'I did. It was the only thing I had that held memories of you.'

Malum' Justice walked in from one of his sessions with the neighbourhood's 'meshuga intellectuals', as my mother called them: 'amadod' ane public opinion', as they called themselves.

'Ya, man! I knew the story was too good to be true!' he exclaimed on seeing Danisile.

The puzzle was slowly coming together. The biggest piece was the smile missing a few teeth, which Danisile flashed at Malum' Justice to acknowledge his elation. That must have been the reason my mother never bothered to fix the guitar after the last cord snapped under the pressure of my fingers during one of my enthusiastic strumming sessions.

'I take it this means we will eventually be restringing that thing then, Ncedi?' Malum' Justice said, motioning to the guitar and throwing the newspaper which he had been squeezing under his armpit onto his rollaway bed.

We all laughed. I must admit, however, that I was not too sure why I was laughing.

What I do know, though, is that at that moment, joy snuck in through our backdoor, and we now had an endless supply of happiness.

From what I could make out of the rest of the conversation between Malum' Justice, Dan and my mother, it seemed that over the years everyone had convinced themselves that Dan had died in exile. Those who were not convinced had forced themselves to kill her in their minds. My mother belonged to the latter.

In reality, Dan had been roaming the streets of countries whose names I had never heard before, and now stood resurrected in our capsule.

'No one helps the dead,' she finally said to stop Malum' Justice from assailing her with his million questions.

After supper, Dan stood up to again announce her intention of leaving. But before she did, she took my mother in her arms and gave her a passionate kiss, as if no one else was in the room. She also took the liberty of releasing the tears she had been holding back from the moment she walked into our house. She thanked us for the meal, pinched my left cheek and winked at me, and then patted Malum' Justice on the back.

'Where will you go?' my mother asked.

'My father's house has many mansions. I'm sure there's a spot somewhere in this world I can call home.'

'How about your people? Where is your brother?' Malum' Justice quizzed her.

'They said not to return to them unless I was married to a man, any man. So, I guess, on my own it will have to be for the longest time,' Dan chimed.

'Stay the night, at least. Besides, it is way too late for you to start looking for a place now,' Ncedi offered her kissing friend.

Dan stayed the night and infinite others afterwards. She restrung the guitar and taught me to play every song she herself knew how to, plus the many new ones we made up together. She became my partner in the pursuit of dreams. In between playing songs, we both indulged in our shared favourite pastime: mind travel. I introduced her to the praying mantis, who let it slip that now that her prayers had been answered, she might not be around for much longer.

Months went by. The mantis stopped its conversations with Gold. Music danced through our home. Malum' Justice found a job as a court interpreter. In the game of musical chairs, we had swapped positions with our neighbours. It was they who now threatened to sue us because of the joyous racket that was known to spill through the cracks of our shack home.

We still did not have much by way of amplitude. The extra money that Malum' Justice made only paid for our meals and firewood.

It was warmer in our hearth. It was warmer in our hearts, too, to be honest. And this is the version that is difficult to admit to. It didn't hurt as much anymore when the kids called me by my nickname. I had concluded that every rock star needed a stage name, and seeing as I was fast becoming one, I reasoned, what better name for a rock legend in the making to have than the name Rock?

69 JERUSALEM STREET

Even the semi-senile in our township knew what month it was, thanks to the ever-present, back-to-back dust volcano eruptions, prancing about as if to a tune played by an arthritic fiddler. August was the month of this spectacle. Whirlwinds came, and like ice skaters, twirled themselves to dizzying frenzies then stopped seconds before blowing everyone away.

I was again reminded, by the whirlwinds of August 9, 1997, that August winds, unlike those of other months, always came armed with a purpose. Four to be exact: shooing children weaving memories off the streets; clearing the same streets of limping three-legged dogs with decaying teeth; applying a layer of crimson on the baby nappies lynched in the yet-to-heat-up spring sun, and plummeting women into a swamp of unrelenting pain. August. That majestic month set aside for the celebration of women.

'Trust them to give us a dirty month,' my mother said.

August, more than any other month, was notorious for its effect on the senses. So much so that it came to live in most women's minds as the vision and smell of a cheery but appalling man with two bags of sliced onions hanging from his armpits.

All of August's days were cruel, but for our reprieve. Saturdays seemed a bit merciful, even though that mercy came at a price. The price being our steadfast adherence to established routines. Any form of deviation from which, however small, was met with the harshest chastisement.

Ours were very simple routines, and as such, ones from which it was almost impossible to deviate. That was until Rasputin Moferefere Kgosana, without consulting anyone, decided to veer away from them and by so doing earned us August's fury. Another way of looking at it – and this observation is a gift delivered by hindsight – is that even before this Saturday, he had always lived amongst us as August's wrath manifest, but had been biding time until that hour, on that Saturday, to reveal himself fully.

Our Saturdays began, always, with a breakfast of magwinya, snoekfish, whatcliver and atchar. Young girls with towels wrapped around their waists grudgingly swept their mothers' yards, rivalling the whirlwinds with the number of dust storms they raised. Some men left their houses for work and some for heaven knows where, to return later the same day. For others, the same hour the next day, if at all. Women with pegs dangling from their pinafores and their young on their backs busied themselves with the week's washing and giving their stoeps a shine so bright it could easily be confused for the sun's beam.

A half-drunk neighbour, still smelling of sleep, strolled over to anyone's fence to talk about the party they had attended the night before. The local priest took a more than ample swig of the blood of Christ, and confused himself about which event to attend first: the funeral or the wedding. A young bride in two minds caught sight of her image in a three-way dressing table mirror and wondered which of her now four selves she would still recognise a few years down the aisle. Cupboards were checked for vanilla essence ahead of the day's anticipated baking. Ausi Sinah and her friends, MaPatronella and Sis' Nomonde, made their way out of their houses to ours to sit on the stoep as they had done every Saturday without fail. 'The Township's Trinity', as everyone called them, to avoid calling each by name. Their friendship so old none of them remembered its beginnings.

As far as I can remember, our mornings repeated themselves like this for the 468 Saturdays I had been alive. The afternoons, too, were consistent. They entailed the return of the men called responsible from work or heaven knows where, to the townships but never to their homes. These would be the same men who had left work, or heaven knows where, at about one o'clock, to congregate at around two at the many shebeens that peppered our township. This, so that they could begin the worship of two of the most sacrosanct Saturday deities, for which shebeens were consecrated sanctuaries: beer and football. Shortly before three, they would make themselves comfortable enough to paste their eyes on the screens that would deliver them their weekly dose of a tension-rousing showdown between victory and loss. Shebeen queens would also ready themselves to charge for beers, both consumed and not. Then the man behind the screen, in the black and white shorts, would blow his whistle and declare the battle commenced.

No one had different expectations for this Saturday which, until half-past three, was rolling out very much like any other before.

Ausi Sinah and her friends had finished baking the scones they would swallow with bits of gossip as they sat on the stoep. Ausi Sinah was our landlady and owner of house number 69 Jerusalem Street, the biggest house in all of

Phomolong. She was the youngest of the three friends and being this side of fifty, they called her 'Maiden'. Although she herself had done precious little to preserve her youthful looks, life and gravity had been very kind to her. She rivalled in agility and good looks many women younger than herself. Looking at her standing next to my mother, one could swear that she was the younger of the two. This, even though my mother was actually fifteen years her junior in earth years. However, my mother was at least a hundred years Ausi Sinah's senior in life experiences.

Slightly older than Ausi Sinah, was Sis' Nomonde, who cut a figure reminiscent of Mary, Mother of God but which time's passage had sadly done its fair share to deconsecrate. In the end she looked just like anyone's mother. What she had lost in her pious looks, though, she had more than made up for with the air she exuded, which she must have inherited from a long lineage of women before her. MaPatronella, the crone, was the eldest and thinnest of them all. Beneath the carpet of her now completely greyed hair she carried the wisdom of four sages. A close look at her hair always had me imagining that an intent baker had dusted her head with particles of icing sugar to give her, her sweet disposition.

Number 69 Jerusalem Street was a space that three families called home. My mother, Ntando; Rasputin Moferefere Kgosana, her husband and ostensibly my father; and myself lived in its garage, a self-contained home in and of itself. MaPatronella had recently moved into one of the backrooms after her children finally managed to tell her in no uncertain terms, that they no longer had room for her in what used to be her house, and their hearts.

Ausi Sinah lived in the main house.

She had extended the house from its matchbox

beginnings, using the small fortune she had amassed through means best left undiscussed. The stoep, however, had always been there. The only alteration that had been made was to extend its width to accommodate the friends' girths which had expanded over the years. She had given the rest of the house big windows so that she could steal herself a lot more yellow sunlight and stir green envy amongst her neighbours, all in one stroke. For good measure, she had built two back rooms and a garage, which, as I have said already, she rented out to her friend and my family. She was entrepreneurial. For her, 69 Jerusalem Street was a small section of earth she took pride in calling her own.

On this particular Saturday, the men in the shebeens were slowly losing their sobriety. There was already so much dust that the women had long given up cursing it for soiling their washing. Rasputin, who had also left in the morning as part of the menfolk's exodus – the section that had left for heaven knows where – was making his way back. He was coming back home. To our house. On a Saturday afternoon! He had never done that before. None of the men in Phomolong did that. He was varying our routines and August would not be pleased.

I was the first to see him making his way over, walking in his hurried gait of three sprints, four heavy trots, and two light strolled paces. He always walked like this when he was in a hurry.

I saw him from the vantage of the garage roof, which is where I lay then. I saw him pull his nose in a disdainful way, the more he approached. He scratched it briefly while he was still a hundred paces or so away from Ausi Sinah's Brasso polished gate. It was the smell of the burning vanilla,

I thought, that disturbed the peace in his nostrils. It could have been anything really; pulling his nose was one of his favourite things to do.

The reason for his rush was delivered to me with that gift of hindsight I mentioned earlier. I should say a mixture of hindsight and gossip, really. A package which, as it went, had it that he had been tipped off by our local police, with whom he was the greatest of friends despite having stood on the wrong side of the law more than once in his life. The tip-off was to the effect that someone was finally coming for his head and that they planned on doing so on this very Saturday. And because of who he was, but mostly what he was – an incorrigible brute – he had managed to make himself many enemies. So, he reckoned his home would be the safest place to spend the rest of this Saturday, or his life.

His entire being, which I still had difficulty reconciling as human at the basest level, and as my father at a more intimate one, took shape. It is probably best I take a bit of time here to explain the sort of person he was, so that maybe you might understand my dilemma.

In a bid to convince me that he was indeed human, my mother had told me more than once that he had come into this world bearing the names Rasputin Moferefere Kgosana as was given to him by his parents, who, as stories had it, were the sweetest creatures to walk the face of this earth. Second only to MaPatronella. Also, to give credence to my mother's story, there was a birth certificate to attest to this tall tale of him as human.

My mother had confessed to not knowing any details about his life until after the moment when he 'bumped into her' in the university alley, on that other dreadful Saturday morning, a little more than nine years ago.

'We did not meet, you see, in that conventional way that people meet,' she said, always with one tear rolling down her left cheek. 'He bumped into me. Ya, he bumped into me,' she would nod, clear her throat, and then take a deep breath before continuing.

Then she would look up to the ceiling, or the sky if she happened to be sitting outside at the time of telling, pretending to survey them for traces of a less harsh version of the story of their meeting. Her runny nose would betray the composure she was trying to maintain, but she would continue.

'Ras, as he was known then, bumped into me at the devil's playground. That dark alley between my res-room and the university pub which was known as "Ko di Heleng". He … uhm … grabbed me from behind and then put his hand over my mouth … to stop me from screaming. As they all do.'

At this point she would make that chuckling sound people make when they are too embarrassed to cry, 'Then he grabbed me by the scruff of my neck and threatened to strangle me if I didn't do as he said. Aargh, then in that space of time way too many things happened. I can't remember half of them, you know?'

She would always be tempted to stop here, but would continue despite herself, as if seized by another presence.

'It lasted,' she would go on, 'say … nine minutes when it happened. But there is not one day that goes by without me feeling his weight on me. That's how you were conceived, you know?' she always concluded, in anticipation of my barrage of questions.

Questions which, incidentally, were the same all the time. I repeated them partly because I really did not understand the choices she had made or, maybe, I should say the choices she was forced to make.

'And abortion … why did you not consider an abortion?' I would ask her, always in the most genuine way. Without sounding as if I was ungrateful for the gift of life she had given me.

'It's one of those things, you know? Easier to talk about than do,' she would say, searching my face for a sign of reassurance. 'Well, there was my father, also. Our customs, my uncles, our religion, and Djeezas to consider.'

For all her education and trained tongue, there was a way in which she said 'Djeezas', that made it sound like she was not talking about the man in the Bible but about another icon or saint equally as holy, only one that lived somewhere in Phomolong.

'My father came up with the solution that was designed to save his face, sell my soul, and protect the family name from shame. That was for me to marry the man he saw no fault in calling the father of my child.'

Our conversation would always end at this point. Partly because she could not bring herself to say any more and partly because, well, I had heard variations of the story from that point on.

But what I have shared with you so far, is the person Rasputin was on the inside. I hope you are beginning to understand my feelings towards him, based as they are, on the fact that he was a man who could easily be said to be hard on the soul. He, sadly, was also hard on the eye. It was as if both his inside and outside had conspired to complete this picture of him as a fiend. His face looked as if it had been put together by someone who had been interrupted and thought he would come back to finish it. Only, at the time when he thought he would, something else more pressing had come up to detract from finishing his work. The result being that Rasputin's nose was left a bit too close to his mouth, and his eyes too close to his hairline.

There were some people who strongly believed that his face was the initial model on which God had practiced making faces, a few days after the beginning of Genesis, when He had not yet perfected the art.

He was also a very big man, with a belly bigger than that of a pregnant elephant. In it he carried all manner of undigested morsels from when he was still a teenager, side-by-side with morsels from the week before. He also carried traces of the first beer he had ever drunk at university. His chest was such that if it were one centimetre wider, anyone looking at him would be forgiven for mistaking it for breasts. In short, he was a very unattractive man.

Many said that it was because he was born wrong that he looked the way he did. What they meant by this only they knew. Some said it explained why, next to Rasputin, Ntando always looked as if she had an albatross hanging around her neck. They, too, knew only too well what they meant. I was more inclined to agree with the latter.

On the stoep, the trinity was on their second pot of rooibos and more scones than they cared to count, all the while wrapped under a blanket of light conversation and the kind of genuine laughter that only people who have known and loved each other for so long could share.

At the stadium, the team in yellow and black gear had scored one goal, leaving the supporters of the team in black and white, also at the stadium, in all the shebeens in Phomolong and elsewhere no doubt, not at all pleased.

Ntando was in the garage now, seriously burning the last batch of scones she had started baking in the morning because she had trailed off to attend to the washing as well.

Rasputin finally walked in through Ausi Sinah's gate and grunted a reluctant greeting to the trinity. They responded, cheerfully as always. He made straight for the refrigerator and grabbed himself the first of the beers he would down in his house. Not even he could tell how many others were already in his system.

I stayed on the roof of Ausi Sinah's house and watched the ants taking it apart one speck at a time. I felt no alarm because I had been watching them do this for years now and was convinced that it would take them at least another thousand before they did any meaningful damage to it. By then, I was certain, Ausi Sinah would have the presence of mind to replace it if she were still alive.

It became clear to me that it was definitely the vanilla essence that was messing with the amity in Rasputin's nose.

Through the biggest ant hole in the roof, I heard him say to my mother in the smuggest voice ever, ' Now, to which god are we offering the scones in the oven?'

My mother did not respond. Not in words in any event. She chose to charge for the stove to remove the burnt scones, which were not much of a loss given that she had already made enough to last us a whole week.

Feeling ignored, Rasputin plonked himself in front of the TV, only to find that his team was losing. At this point, however, he was not too stressed, or if he was, he was hiding it very well. It was still the first half of the match and in his left hand he held the beer he had just fished out of the fridge, in his right, a yet to be opened pack of cigarettes, and in his heart, the hopes that the second half would bring his team victory. At the back of his head sat the suspicion that if his would-be killers were the determined sort, they would think nothing of making true their threat before the day was over.

He lit his first cigarette when the man in the black and white shorts blew his whistle to signal the end of the first half. Ntando took out the ironing board to prepare for the already dried washing. Shebeen queens filled tables with beers that had been ordered and more that had not in response to the suggestive adverts that always came on during half time.

The trinity spoke about the present and the past as if the two belonged to the same era, making distinctions only where life-defining moments were concerned. If they had been in the habit of talking about the future, who is to say that they would not have spoken about it or even stopped the life-changing moment which was brewing in their backyard.

Moferefere got up and made for the fridge to get his second beer. By this time he had already smoked three cigarettes; he was known to chain smoke whenever his nerves were shot.

He made his way back to his seat in time to see the man in the black and white shorts blow his whistle again to command the start of the second half of the showdown. The men in the sheebens whispered frenzied calls for silence, bracing themselves for the same second half. In the middle of the second half, when the score had changed again and put the team in the yellow and black gear in a two-nil lead, souring Moferefere's mood and that of other supporters of the team in black and white wherever they may have been, Ntando brought the ironing board to the section of the garage we called the living room, where Rasputin sat. Although, in earnest, the garage could easily have been called 'the everything room'.

Ntando cast a quick glance at the Djeezas standing on the room divider, behind the artificial roses above the TV, and asked Rasputin as she pulled the ironing board open, 'Who's winning?'

A question, which, if she had held off asking for five seconds, would have been answered by the commentator's voice instead of the bark she received from her husband. The Djeezas on the room divider did not seem affected in any way by what the commentator or Rasputin had just said. He kept that placid look for which room divider Djeezases are renowned. The final whistle blew halfway through Ntando's ironing. In the shebeens, grown men cried as they had never done before, not even at their own mothers' funerals. It should be said though that it was not all the men that cried, only some of the supporters of the team in black and white, and amongst those that cried, very few cried over the actual loss. Most cried over the money they had lost in the bets made earlier.

The trinity heard the score blaring over an ill-tuned radio and paid it very little attention. There were only ten cigarettes left in Rasputin's packet and his sour mood had now curdled. Ntando was folding one of his white shirts. I was growing bored with the ants and was readying myself to come down from the roof. The sun was saying its goodbyes.

Rasputin got up for his third beer and on his way to the fridge he deliberately bumped into an obviously excited Ntando, whose team had just won. Through his actions he was looking to start trouble and at the time, little did he know that he would succeed. When he came back from the fridge he stopped behind her and asked why it was that she was so happy, when for him it was such a sad day. Ntando, not knowing that he was not only talking about the soccer but also about the news he had received earlier and had until now managed to force to the recesses of his mind, continued to fold his white shirt with no response, just a smile on her face. He started to raise his voice and hurled such insults at her, concerning her mother. Instead of an answer to his question, she felt herself seized by something outside of herself, tentatively holding her back. Thinking that no one had a right to throw up such vitriol on account of a team's loss, Ntando spoke back to him as vociferously, perhaps for the first time in her life. He didn't take kindly to that and raised the bottle in his hand, aiming for her head.

She saw this and pulled it out of his hand. This was easy to do because although this was his fourth beer in his house, it was growing evident that he'd had a couple more at that heavens knows where place he had been to earlier.

I remember the look of horror on his face when he realised that she was clearly not following the script he had read off other men who told of what happened when they beat up their wives.

According to this script, this was the point where Ntando was supposed to cover her face and prepare to let out a symphony of sounds as each of his blows landed on her body.

August stood at our home's threshold and, by the look of things, was not pleased.

Ntando stood in the middle of the room with the same look on her face of the room divider Djeezas behind the artificial roses. Rasputin, because he was so drunk and riddled with all manner of fears, raised his hand to her for what would be the last time in his life. She had the help of the iron, the bottle in her hand, her body and the courage she had felt steaming inside her, delivered from a place deep inside herself that she did not even know existed.

The trinity heard the scuffle but got to it when it was too late for them to do anything. By the time they got to where August had stood earlier, Rasputin was no more.

Again, Ntando was about to lose her freedom. Only this time, she would be moved to a smaller prison. A move which would eventually free her of the farce of her life up to that point, and all the illusions of freedom she had belligerently clung to.

'Forgive us our just passes, as we forgive them that just chance pass against us,' I thought I heard her say, as she was led to the yellow van that would deliver her to her new life.

It is only now, short of my twentieth year, reminiscing about 69 Jerusalem Street, that I realised what she actually said.

'Forgive us our trespasses as we forgive them that trespass against us.'

THE GLASSPECKER

The telltale sign that almost gave her away was the hazy gaze she gave the final smoulder of the cigarette whose dying spark almost kissed her knuckles. She held it loosely, dangling between her pinkie and ring finger, whilst her thumb busied itself caressing her middle finger, as she always did when her mind drifted away. Had it not been for the sudden strong whiff of cinnamon that filled the room and sent messages to Mandla's strong hand – which he placed on her shoulder – she might have burned herself.

'Nonceba, uyasha,' his voice brought her back to her body, long enough for her to kill the cigarette, but not to disturb whatever was on her mind.

'Cinnamon … Hmm, must be a special occasion.' A whisper murmured from no particular face.

And it was. The old year had just passed the baton on to the new and deposited half-a-bag-full of hope in everyone's drunken hearts. Except for hers. Apart from me, no one at that point knew that the last day of the year had also placed half-a-bag-full of something else into Nonceba's heart. And her mind, in a feeding frenzy, had already doubled it in size.

The cigarette in question had been lit five and a half minutes before the end of the year and smoked in the most unusual way any of her friends had seen her do, without the obligatory story that went with it, or the close-to-command offer to take a puff. Counting this one, she had smoked a hundred and three of them in total. This added up because her regular group of friends had heard the story a hundred and two times already, because there had been exactly a hundred and two special occasions in her life since she discovered this flavour. Everyone at The Devil's Bottom knew the story and was in the habit of reciting the end of it with her every time she told it. So that it became somewhat of a soundtrack to the smoking.

'… the person who introduced me to these cigarettes is the most extraordinary person I have ever met,' the story always ended.

It was accented by a heavy slur and an emphasis on the word 'I' followed by two knocks on the chest, a bite of the lower lip and an overenthusiastic nod. A confusing gesture indeed. First time hearers of the story could be seen mostly by the puzzled look on their faces, brought on by their attempt to make out who the subject of praise in the sentence was, herself of the 'extraordinary person'. It was never clear. The first day of the new year was not even half an hour old when she felt her palate belligerently accosted by the lingering aftertaste of a life lived in haste. Perhaps this was why she hadn't finished her cigarette. She took a swig of the Stroh Rum she had been downing all evening and silently prayed that it would cleanse her palate. It didn't.

There was a rat-like smile plastered on the face of one of the scavenging cats that always hovered about, sniffing-sniffing at The Devil's Bottom. A night like this was the jackpot. He didn't even have to exert himself, his prey practically landed – garnish and all – in his claws. He wasn't choosy either, he polished off whatever the night provided.

Nonceba and her friends were amongst the most regular patrons at The Devil's Bottom, so much so that they were known by name. She, specifically, was known by more than one. Her ordinarily rambunctious personality resulted in this burden of many names, one for every occasion. All used to describe her predilections, more than distinguishing her from the others. Most of them, however, were used liberally behind her back.

The most consistent thing she was called was 'Our Lady of Mercy', for short. An unfortunate coincidence, given that this nickname approximated what her real names suggested when translated or subjected to interpretation. Her real names were Nonceba Mary, accompanied by a surname so lenient it didn't demand a space in anyone's memory (this, according to those who made everyone's business theirs, and there were plenty of those). On the very rare occasion that there was enough collective sober thought at The Devil's Bottom to allow for the utterance of full sentences, she was addressed as 'Our Lady of Mercy Who Shed Her Clothes Because She Felt Pity'. She had earned the name for her tendency to take unworthy men to bed because she felt sorry for them.

The first day of January 2005 found her sitting at a brassy table with three of her dearest friends, staring at a presence that only she could see, making senseless murmurs which only she and the apparition seemed to understand. It put a smile on my face. For her friends within earshot, who later would become the sole bearers of the misfortune of having to tell the story at least a hundred and three times, her mumblings seemed to have been about loss and the sense of grief it brought on.

To see someone mourn so deeply all the things they never quite possessed was mystifying. But, then again, one reaches a point in life when the screen of mist that separates memory from the present and the future is torn in two, to allow for clarity of mind never known before. I relished the knowledge that my mind had finally been released from the prison house of time, and set free to roam wherever it pleased, unbound. I smiled again, but I doubt she saw that.

She mourned the loss of her youth. The first day of the year was also the day she was born. On this day, 30 years ago, she had made her entry into the world. But, because she had practically given birth to herself in the streets of Johannesburg, she had been forced to learn how to be mother, father, aunt, and cousin to herself, all at once. So, even though she had just turned 30 and felt herself no longer young, she had never really been young.

She mourned the fact that the cinnamon cigarette she had held between her fingers was her last. No one in Johannesburg sold them, they only had cherry tobacco here. Her extraordinary friend from Egypt had hinted that it was becoming increasingly difficult to send more given the latest developments in her own life.

She mourned the loss of her life, which, even though she had not completely lost it at this point, was as good as lost. She had lived it as though she had borrowed it from someone to whom she had no intentions of ever returning it intact. She had never really cared for the newness of things, the things she really enjoyed were those that had been pre-owned and discarded by others.

This explained her wardrobe of second-hand items – vintage clothing as she preferred to call it. It explained her smile, a display so immaculate it belonged on the face of the child she had tried but failed to be. It explained her predilection to pick food from other people's plates, so that in the entire time she had been to The Devil's Bottom, not a single meal had ever been charged to her bill. It explained her knowledge of the world gleaned from second-hand books highlighted and underlined by ghostly hands to which she had no affinities. And it explained her popularity at The Devil's Bottom, particularly with the sort of cat that described himself as being in between marriages.

Her search for ideas to calm her boiling mind turned her face, in desperation, to her right where Mandla sat. She stared at him steadfastly, plunging in through his bloodshot eyes and burrowing into the depths of his mind in search of answers. She didn't find any. No doubt Mandla had a lot of answers, just none that answered the kind of questions buzzing in her head.

It was no surprise that Mandla was the first person to whom she turned. Mandla, her on and off (mostly off) lover, had an air about him. As if he had seen Jesus' toes or the Dalai Lama's Calvin Klein underpants or something. A residual, perhaps, from when he used to be principal vicar at the Seventh Day Adventist of the Brotherhood of Men and Women Who Worshiped on Sundays: the SDABMWWWS. When the church defrocked him for his tendency of dipping his fingers in the collection basket to finance his Saturday drinking sprees, they had left his priestly aura intact. His 'springboard'. He used to boast about successfully launching himself as a 'freelance spiritual entrepreneur', sole founder and member of 'Mandl'enkosi Spiritual and Entrepreneurship Consultants at Your Service'.

He catered mostly to the newly rich interested in getting their hands on the next big deal and a backstage pass to heaven – in that order. Impeccable though his answers may have been, sandwiched as they were between mounds of guilt, seamless reams of greed and a leaf of remorse, none were of any use to Our Lady of Mercy.

Then she turned to her left, where Mkhokheli, her oldest friend and fellow pilgrim through the valleys of disappointment and failure, was sitting. Now, where Mandla exuded a heavenly air, Mkhokheli had one reminiscent of the sum total of all the overacted characters in every badly written soapie there ever was. He fancied himself a poet. His choice of vocation was also a badly formulated ruse to compensate for his lack of common sense. His mind was never in his head, and when he had occasion to say anything – drunk or sober – he let out a salvo of babble that only he was in the habit of calling 'poetry'. He had a way of saying 'poetry', with his head bobbing from side to side, that made the word sound like shit. As usual, his 'mind was out of his head hunting for his soul', as he habitually declared when he realised that not even he understood what he had said. It surprised her little that he would be of no use.

'Tsk, why did I bother?' she shook her head.

Her final hope, she hoped against hope, would come from the girl, Hope, who was sitting in front of her. But Hope, the girl with the unsightly habit of carrying leftover sleep in the drooping bags under her squint marble eyes, was hopeless. At the exact moment when Our Lady of Mercy's eyes met Hope's, she found that hope had transformed itself into a vision of an overly exploited proletariat zombie that belonged to a union which had long lost its vigour.

She asked Mkhokheli for a regular cigarette. He seemed

to understand her request and gave her one. She lit it herself with the only matchstick in her box that still had fire in it. She took a deep drag until she felt the smoke dancing on her lips, pushing to visibility the lines of latitude which time had etched on her forehead to give her a semi-perpetual frown.

Hope was the youngest member of the group, and the way in which she regurgitated everything she had ever read gave the impression that she had a secret well of knowledge hidden somewhere inside her. But it soon became clear that what Hope had in carefully crafted erudition, she lacked in experience. And besides, today her sole interest appeared to lie in the twin preoccupation of peddling her invented memories for as many drinks as possible, so that she could dig a pool deep enough to drown her imagined sorrows. She did this deliberately, drinking to forget. She had pontificated before about the meaninglessness of drinking to forget, and a great many other things.

'Wham! Next morning,' she said, reaching a level of animation that only she was capable of, 'there they are. Those sorrows you were eagerly trying to drown, twice the size they were the previous night, and sprawled right next to you in the discomfort of your crowded bed!'

She was very articulate, but that, too, was of no use to Our Lady of Mercy right now. Hope kept bobbing her head to the phantom tune of 'Live for the Moment', rapped by a squeaky voice at the back of her head.

The lack of answers and the cigarette Mkhokheli had given Nonceba intensified her craving for one last cinnamon cigarette. It wasn't until she broke down and cried that her friends managed to extricate themselves from their joint and individual temporary insanities.

'What kind of city is this that has no cinnamon cigarettes?!'

she yelled, as if raising a question concerning life and death.

'Cherry tobacco, Ncebs. Cherry tobacco is a good alternative,' Hope said, trying to mask the irritation in her voice.

Her irritation was understandable, given that Our Lady of Mercy had let her yell out at the exact moment that one of Hope's most elaborate invented memories to date was reaching crescendo.

No one else said anything.

At ten past one, she asked Mkhokheli for another cigarette. He put one in her hand and kissed her left cheek. She got up without ceremony and staggered out of The Devil's Bottom like a silent fart, never to return.

I followed her before the salivating rat-cat standing next to the door could say anything to her. I walked slowly behind her, making sure that my footsteps did not startle her. When I was comfortably near enough I leaned forward and reminded her of the first day we met. She smiled, pushing back the tears. I smiled back, only because I didn't know what else to do.

'Remember, Nonceba, how we pretended we were Nefertiti and Nzinga making love across timelines? You said it was "a bad comparison and downright sacrilegious." I said it didn't matter, what mattered was that we felt like the greatest African queens in "post-cloital" glow. Remember how you laughed at the word cloital? Remember, also, how you kissed my forehead in a fit of laughter and told me you quite liked that word, "cloital". I loved how you said it in that fake English accent of yours, heavily laden with your Xhosa accent.

"I hope you will find time to send it, like you had

threatened, to the people who update the Collins dictionary. Wouldn't it be fun to flick through the pages of the dictionary and be greeted by that word, cloital? Explained as "the magical act of mutual sexual stimulation between two women, where both women pleasure each other unselfishly until their bodies and emotions are dancing to the same beat". Cloital. I had never laughed so hard in my whole life!'

I rambled on but she kept walking. Not having a body has its disadvantages.

'We were magic in every sense,' she chuckled, as she used her tongue to clear the snot from her upper lip.

'Remember, also, how you said that I was the only person who had been patient enough to find their way into your heart,' I continued, hoping she would answer.

She didn't.

She looked back, expecting to see my face, I guess. I hoped.

She only felt the wave of an early morning breeze brush across her face when I reached over to touch her. I could see by the way she bit her lower lip that she knew I was there. I had seen her bite her lower lip like that a couple of times in Egypt.

She walked a couple more paces, opened her car door, got inside and put the key in the ignition but didn't start it until she had let out the sob she had been holding back since midday, the time when the couriered package from Egypt had arrived.

I guess I had not given enough thought to the contents of the package. I had put in it a poem I had written for her, despite her having called me 'the stuffiest Egyptian' she had ever met.

I called it 'Nzinga's Flame'. I also put in a stone from the last site my team had excavated, and a note written in haste.

Dear Nonceba,

Egypt is beautiful. For how long, I don't know. Isis sent me a message. Can't make sense of it but something in the way it is written suggests I can't ignore it. I feel compelled to act on it. It's a lot of gibberish, really, but it rings in my head so loudly I have to silence it by responding. Every day I am haunted by what you said when you left, with a promise to return as soon as you had sorted out your life down there, remember? I guess it was more complicated than I thought. It was true what you said, sometimes the things that seem the most natural to do, are often the most impossible.

But, Nonceba, I am afraid there are two things I feel myself no longer capable of. I can't wait any more, nor can I continue the work of exhuming love from your heart. Remember how you said you felt as though I had worked like a meticulous glasspecker in the way I opened your heart to let love in? Remember? Well, I am afraid even if I was able to wait, the way things are in my mind right now, I would be at risk of shattering your heart to pieces, pecking away at it.

Please don't hate me. I feel I must do what I need to do. If Isis permits, or rather, Osiris, or both of them, I will see you in the afterlife. I'll come visit soon, but I'm afraid I can no longer send you those cinnamon cigarettes you love so much.

Love always,
The Glasspecker.
PS: Good luck with your life, mine ran out.

I don't know which set the breakdown on, the letter or the poem. If I had known, I would not have sent her the package. She had not written in such a long time, I thought she had forgotten about me. I thought I had just become a footnote in the story of her life, a regular supply of cinnamon cigarettes.

I knew life had shown her many things, hard and beautiful, but what I had not counted on was the effect this package – which had flown from the top of the continent, dragging years of sorrow in its wake – would have on her.

When she finally decided to start her car, it was, first, in the direction of the nearest filling station. She bought herself a neon-coloured tow rope, R28, and a pack of cherry tobacco, R22.

'Eish, you mean to tell me I have to roll this myself?' I heard her ask the half-asleep petrol station cashier.

'Yebo, sisi,' he said in a singsong voice, eager to be left alone. 'But you are going to need paper for that. Do you want me to ring it up for you?'

'Yes, please do,' she said. 'While you're at it, why don't you throw in that writing pad?' she pointed at the one with a picture of Mary mother of Jesus, with a naughty girlish smile on her face.

'Sixty-eight rand, zonke, sisi," he said.

She put a R100 note in his hand and flashing him Mary's smile, she said, 'Keep the change.'

When she got home, she sat on the dining table and made a dismal attempt of rolling herself a cherry cigarette, while she sang the song her mother had sung the day after her father died.

Lelizwe linomoya, baba ngesab' umoya
Shiya baba, ngesab' umoya
Linomoya baba, ngesab' umoya

She sat down to scribble her last thoughts and when she was done, got up on the table to offer her life, a living sacrifice to whichever god cared enough to receive it.

When they finally found her note, later that same day, it was placed neatly under the stone excavated from Egypt, her feet dangling loosely above it. Hope read it out loud for everyone.

Dear All,

I'm sorry I did not have enough time to write each of you an individual note, but here's what I want to say. I could no longer bear living in a city that had no cinnamon cigarettes. I tried cherry tobacco, Hope, but they are not quite the same. You can have the rest of the packet. Tell Mandla to marry Zo or go back to Ntokozo and stop messing with their heads. In fact, tell all the boys at The Bottom who are contemplating putting themselves in other people's marriages to do the same. I'm afraid I won't be around to offer my services anymore.

Burn everything I own, my body even. But first, douse it in cinnamon oil. Don't cry at my funeral. Move on with your lives. Find happiness in your own hearts. I have gone to join the extraordinary glasspecker with an endless supply of my kind of smokes.

If keeping me in your hearts is not enough, and only if you must, open a tobacco shop. And oh, be sure to stock it full of cinnamon cigarettes, I'll come visit sometime for a smoke or a chat.

I had tried talking her out of it, but no sooner had I opened my mouth had she been sitting next to me, right on Nefertiti's tomb, blowing smoke rings into the air.

Confessions of Karelina

The thing about second, third and even fourth opinions, is the way they often drag one through a morass of unnecessary blah-blahs, back to that all too familiar destination called conviction. And because she suffered from that malady called falling in lust, she found that she needed as many opinions as she could reject, before finally deciding to go with her initial impulse.

Correctly so, because it was caprice in the first place, that had drawn her to this place where her mind and soul were now engaged in a protracted argument about the sinfulness of her doings. Her soul said 'Sin!' while her mind calmly disagreed, both leaving the argument unresolved.

The decision to seek a fifth opinion streamed into her room with the rays of morning sunshine which, for her, also marked the end of the soul searching vigil she'd had with her conscience. She didn't know then that it would take three more unhelpful opinions as well as an almost humiliating one, before she'd revert to the conviction her mind had whispered to her, ever so quietly. Because honestly, really, truly honestly, what she had done was not sinful. She had simply fallen in love.

But because she was Catholic – even if only through indoctrination, by confirmation day she had claimed for herself the right to become part of one of the world's largest religious institutions, with an enormous capacity for guilt thrown in as a bonus.

Yet, she couldn't help ruminating on the words of that Sufi poet who once wrote about love and lovemaking: that both were akin to touching God.

How true the mystic's words rang in her head! She tried to convince herself – in that part of her conscience still uncontaminated by Catholic guilt – that in Dana's arms the night before, she had indeed touched God. Dana, with a smile so real, so compelling, it would be difficult for even the most austere bride of Christ to resist. Dana, with hands so tiny, so tender, so filled with magic. Dana, scattering petals of pleasure on every part of her, with every touch. Dana, ladder to heights never before imagined. Dana …

With one half of her face attempting a smile, and the other releasing a sigh, she remembered how she was often prone to hyperbole and tried to rein in her thoughts.

Once again, she tried to sleep. But, in both mind and body, she tossed and turned, flooded by thoughts of Dana. She thought about how quickly Dana – using just one hand – had managed to remove her bra. Jesus Maria! She thought of the warmth of Dana's breath between her breasts, and how beautiful it felt, even though she'd never done that sort of thing before – well, not with a woman. Mother of all saints in heaven! She saw her again in her mind's eye, kneeling at her feet, moments before she came for the first time in her life.

She tried again to banish these thoughts and the delight they came wrapped in. Then, recalling how the catechism had helped her before to abandon her carnal thoughts, she got up from her bed to find it and read it, so that she could rid herself of this glee.

Flicking through its pages, she searched for the section where she vaguely remembered the confession rituals being. She read them at least three times before liberally editing each one in line with her still pronounced confusion. The thought of looking for a rosary to complete this performance of piety darted through her mind, but not feeling too pressed by it, she ignored the urge.

Then she went on her knees and turned her gaze heavenward, from where she hoped her comfort would come, but instead, her gaze met the whitewashed concrete slab that was the ceiling of her ground floor townhouse unit. On it she spotted the fly that had been buzzing around her ear for the past hour, taking a break. She postponed her attempt at prayer to attend to the more pressing mission of condemning said fly to a not-so-gentle death. Having gotten murder out of the way, she returned to the business of prayer.

'Uhm, Lord, I think I am sorry for having offended thee,' she said with certainty the size of a grain of rice. 'But I hope you understand that, right now, I can't make my mind up if indeed I have,' she continued with even less fervour. 'I detest all my sins but as I said, right now, I can't make up my mind if this would count among them,' she went on, chuffed at her seamless editing of the prayer. 'Because of thy just punishment, but most of all because I know that all my other sins, the ones I can put my finger on, that is,' here she paused, realising just how bad a pun that was, 'they offend thee, who art all good and deserving of all my love,' she ended with feigned persuasion.

At this point she sensed herself slipping into an abyss of mental images where all she could see were fingers. Hers. Dana's. Sometimes Dana's and hers, and at other times still, theirs together. Fingers touching, fingers clutching, fingers tracing the sides of necks. Fingers navigating bodies, fingers moving from shoulders and across warm breasts. Fingers journeying downwards around belly buttons, crosswise around shoulder blades, down spines. Fingers scratching and then resting briefly on torsos. Fingers stroking ankles, fingers travelling at high speed up the sides of anticipating thighs, hair follicles standing to attention in their wake. Fingers circling pubic areas: slippery, shaky fingers looking, searching, for the house of pleasure. Fingers fondling vulvas, fingers massaging, caressing each desire-filled nerve. Fingers licked. Fingers wiping away sweat. Fingers pointing her back to prayer. Fingers now firmly clasped in prayer.

She gasped and composed herself enough to continue, 'I firmly resolve, with the help of thy grace, to sin no more, and to avoid the near occasion of sin. Although I can't say for sure about this one, which, if you have been following my reasoning – and I know you have – I still can't say for sure if it was sin.'

Here she closed her eyes and wondered if crossing herself would be a good idea. But before she could decide, her Catholic fingers had already gone ahead and made the sign of the cross.

As she neared the end of her prayer, she rearranged her face to a facsimile of piety, 'In the name of the Father, the Son and the … uhhmm … Holy Spirit. Amen.'

But still, she could not fall asleep.

So she did what all guilt ridden insomniacs do. She reached for a bottle of Merlot without bothering with a wine glass. Then she got hold of her phone and called Thato, her friend of twenty years, whose advice – for its sobriety – she found useless. Then she called her sister, whose preachy suggestions she found even less useful. Finally, she tried

Dana, her accomplice, whose advice she found too lustful and for reasons quite different from the others, equally unhelpful. She could have gone on in this vein forever, but for the realisation that she had run out of airtime and wine all at once.

In the morning, one pounding headache and a pair of puffy eyes later, just enough airtime to send an SMS for a plea to be called back, and four rays of Thursday morning sunlight sliding through her blinds, she found herself just as far from resolving her dilemma as she'd been the night before. She found that she still had no idea whether the contrition she'd shared her bed with had been a valid act of penitence or just an extended guilt trip.

Her next move was to find a fifth opinion. But this, she realised, she'd have to delay until her head had registered its last throb, and her body had readied itself to be hauled out of bed without the threat of last night's dinner landing on the floor. She would get the fifth opinion by consulting a higher power. Or, perhaps more aptly, an agent of a higher power: a Father. Not her sperm father – matters of the heart always eluded this father of hers. But a Father, with a capital letter F, of the Catholic persuasion, the sort that wear white collars and walk around in dresses on Sundays.

Her body was more forgiving than her head. After several attempts at sitting up, she eventually managed without any threat of regurgitation. And then she made the all-important decision that would govern her day. She decided that, ready or not, her head had no choice but to tag along to the fifth opinion, and if necessary, she'd have to help it along with an aspirin or two. Or ten.

She swallowed two litres of water to flush out the wine still coursing through her veins. She stepped into the shower and started rehearsing the opening lines that experience reminded her she would have to deliver. She did this to the soundtrack of the shower and the white noise playing in her head.

'Forgive me, I have sinned.' The words tasted a tad bland, like they needed a little more something. 'Forgive me, big brother, for I have sinned.' This one sounded like something from a reality TV show conceived by someone with a rolled-up ten rand note stuck up his nose. She tried three more variations before the words from her devout Catholic past eventually came to her.

Forgive me, Father, for I have sinned. The line she had rehearsed all morning rang in her head.

Yet, when the time came for her to open her mouth and actually say it, something altogether different came out: 'Forgive me, Father, for I think I may have sinned and I hope I'm wrong.'

Before the priest could open his mouth to say anything, she continued, resting her still-pounding head against the partition that separated piety from transgression: 'I guess you could say more than penance, what I'm really after is your opinion.'

Through the screen, she could see his blurred outline sink back into the chair, pull his left leg over his right and fleck imaginary fluff from the hem of his cassock. Then she heard him clear his throat as he appeared to brace himself for what he hoped would be an interesting session.

'Father,' she said, speaking as if half-addressing God and half-addressing the figure on the other side of the screen, 'how does one decide what constitutes sin?'

'Well, to begin with, there's one's conscience,' he replied

curtly. 'Failing which, there are the precepts clearly stated in the scriptures and the catechism, which, if heeded, help us – as every good Catholic should know – keep from the occasion of sin,' he said, clearly casting aspersions.

'Yes, Father, I know about precepts and everything. But how do I know in my heart of hearts if an act really is sin, when other readings,' – here she was thinking of that Sufi poet – 'suggest differently?'

Beginning to show signs of vexation, he retorted, 'I may be wrong but I suspect, young lady, that there is a point you want to lead me to. Which, I'm afraid, if we continued in this way – devoid of detail as it is – might lead us both to confusion. We would not want that now, would we? So why don't I suggest a different approach,' he went on. 'Why don't you tell me precisely what brings you here, and then maybe we can take it from there?'

He didn't know that in his bid to get clarity, he was sending himself down a slippery slope.

'Oh, okay, I see your point. Well, to start at the beginning, Father, the whole thing started with peas.'

'P's?' he asked, somewhat perplexed as he scrolled down the catalogue of sins he kept at the back of his mind and failing at finding one beginning with the letter P. Intrigued, he then asked, 'What sort of sin begins with pee?'

'No, Father, peas. You know, the round green vegetable? The kind Tsipane loved more than anything on this, God's precious earth, with no shortage in it of things to love.'

He got the point about peas, but again, found himself at a loss over who Tsipane was.

'Well, it was not really about peas, but this woman. Her name is Dana,' she continued.

He now found himself having to contend with two

mysterious characters, where before, there had been only one.

He let out his first fatherly, 'Yes?' A device taught to all priests at the seminary to keep any confession moving.

She picked up her narrative, once more, from the point where it seemed to make sense to her, 'Well, Dana is this woman at work. She works in the cafeteria. She doesn't really work there permanently. She's just standing in for this other guy, whose name I don't know.'

The priest released his second, 'Yes?'

'Well, right from the beginning, Dana was kind of odd … like, in the way she couldn't speak to me. And it was only me she couldn't speak to, you know? She spoke to everyone else, and found no difficulty in saying "Next" or "What will it be today?" But no, not to me. Every time I walked up in the queue, I would see her lips moving but not a sound would come out of her mouth, Father.

'So, I guess you could say she started to speak to me with her ladle. Soon enough everyone – but mostly Tsipane – started noticing that my plate had more peas than anyone else's. Which everyone deciphered before I did: this meant that she liked me.'

'Yes, yes,' he replied uncomprehendingly.

'So, one spoon meant "I like you", and two meant "I really like you". Well, enough about peas, Father. The real point here, is that two nights ago she showed up at my door – uncannily, this – after weeks of me dreaming of her doing just that. She showed up, Father, can you believe it?

'How she got there, what she wanted, how she knew where I lived – these were all questions in my mind, but ones I didn't bother asking her. Instead, I let her in. So, she came in and sat on the couch. I offered her tea, she offered to help me make it. I took out the cups, the milk, everything, you know? I put the kettle on and the room started steaming up. She sat silently.

'You must remember, Father, up until now, silence, this not saying anything to each other, was something I was used to with her. She'd never said much to me at work, so why would I expect her to say any more in my kitchen?'

'Yes, yes, yes,' he replied.

'Well, anyways, the kettle boiled, and those lips I'd been dreaming of for days were right in front of me. Did I mention, Father, that even before she called at my door I'd dreamt of her lips and how I'd love to kiss them? Did I also mention, Father, that she has these lips that scream, "Kiss me!" Well, there they were that night, these lips of my dreams, standing right there in my kitchen, screaming the same message. I had two choices: either ask her all the questions I'd meant to ask as she walked in, or respond to what her lips were screaming at me.

'But before my mind was made up, she came up behind me and whispered into my ear, "I'm not really that fond of tea." Father, you have never heard the word "tea" said with such grace. Tea – Jesus, Father, tea.

'I think to myself, well she is not that fond of tea and I have this second choice. So, what do I do? I turn around, Father. By now she is standing so close to me I can feel her breath on my face – one step closer and I am in her arms. Then she moves and right there, I'm in her arms. Those lips so close, so close!

'Her smell: a mix of jasmine and sandalwood, I think. Then I feel it, her hand on my back. I know now what's about to happen, I know, I know, I know. Part of me screams, "Stop! What about Tsipane?" Tsipane is … well, was … my boyfriend. But before I could answer the question, our lips were touching, and oh, Father, what tender lips. So now we are standing in my kitchen, her lips on mine, tongues touching. Gently. Our tongues are exchanging silent words. Then her hand reaches under my T-shirt, which slips off my body with very little resistance. Now she is nudging me backwards into my bedroom. Then, touch! Father, the sort I had never experienced before. I found in her fingers such magic, such ecstasy. And I asked myself, "Have I just touched God?"'

The priest let out a sigh that filled the confessional with the smell of whiskey. She stopped in her tracks, realising that she may have got carried away. But the he would not allow this. At his insistence, and with the patience of an anatomy lecturer, she went on to describe the things that the woman she now called the 'Mother Teresa of the Sheets' had done to parts of her body she had not known existed.

She paused for a while and wondered if the priest himself had ever touched God. She sensed rising from him such sadness, but also heard him pull himself to an erect position to regain composure. Then, through the screen, she caught a glimpse of him relieving his right leg of the burden of carrying his left as he changed positions.

While he busied himself thus, Karelina proceeded to confound him even more by asking, 'How could this be sin, Father, when after years of trying to touch God, I finally managed to do just that in Dana's arms?'

He heaved a final sigh and gave the crucifix around his neck a gentle rub as he grappled with what to say next.

Finally, he decided on skipping the next step in the confession ritual: the performance of an act of penance. Instead, he went straight to the part where he absolved her of 'sin'.

He began his prayer: 'God, the Father of mercies, who has reconciled the world to himself and sent the Holy Spirit among us for the forgiveness of sins, if this indeed be sin,' Karelina thought she heard him chuckle before continuing 'through the ministry of the Church, may God give you pardon and peace.' Then he paused to take a gulp of air before whispering, 'And right now, I'm doing the best I can to absolve you of your sins, which, I must also add right now, I'm not too certain are sins, after all.' Then, with more composure, he concluded, 'In the name of the Father, and of the Son and of the Holy Spirit. Give thanks to the Lord, for he is good. Amen.'

At the end, Karelina left the confessional with the same befuddled look on her face as she had coming in, though on her body a different message could be read. It was clear to anyone looking that the word 'anticipation' was written all over her.

Understandably, because Dana's last words before she left two nights before were, 'See you again, soon.'

THE READER

This week couldn't have been shittier even if Satan had designed it with the sole intention of torturing me. First, my mother, and now KG. Just when I was trying to do everything by the book. I'm really good at reading things, or so I'd like to think. If I were asked to say what I am, I would say I am a reader. I read situations, I read auras, I read people, I read the Tarot – although I must confess, I'm not too good at this, but still, I do it. I read numbers, all numbers, –and this I'm pretty good at. And sometimes, just sometimes, when the spirit moves me, I read the bones. Although, by right, I shouldn't because I'm not yet done with ukuthwasa, and I know that when I do this I'm traipsing into terrain I shouldn't be trampling on, not just yet.

My mother's passing, at least, was not too much of a surprise. She had been ill, on and off, for a while now. Still, I thought we were going through the 'off' phase and that we would be for a while to come. Even though it didn't surprise me much I didn't see it coming. KG's arrest, on the other hand, is the kind of tosh I couldn't have read even if all my senses were on full alert. She's been out of my life now and not within the radius of people my antennae are adapted to picking up. Unless they're paying, of course. We broke up three months earlier – her decision not mine – and I'd still been trying to come to terms with accepting that whole debacle. When she developed a temperament like that, I can't tell you. When we were still together, she was tiny, scrawny, geeky KG, with a predisposition that rendered her incapable of doing any harm to anyone. How she managed to get herself arrested for beating up a man twice her size, splitting his lip and breaking all the fingers on his right hand in the process, is something that still baffles me.

The charge sheet, as it was read in court, said the standard: Assault with Intent to Cause Grievous Bodily Harm. What she told me was different, though.

She told me, 'I had to let that guy know just how it felt to be humiliated in public, like he was doing to that woman.'

'What woman, what guy?' I asked.

She was scant on the details but secretly, I was proud of her. That was my ex for you, ever involving herself in things that did not necessarily have anything to do with her. Ever the Good Samaritan, ever the voice of the unheard. The fist for the fistless, I didn't think she had that in her.

So now I need money. Lots of it, too. And very quickly if I'm going to be able to give my mom a decent send off and get KG out of jail in time for her to help organise the whole thing. I need to get my hands on a tidy sum. Of the two of us, KG is more expert at these kinds of things, logistics and getting things into action. Me, not as much. To be frank , KG is the only person who's like family to me. I need her now, perhaps more than I've ever needed her.

With my mom's passing I'll have no more family. It will be just me in the world. And with KG and I apart, I'll really have no one. As messed up as this whole thing is, it presents a win-win for everyone. Fact is, I need KG as much as she needs me because, like me, she too has no one. At least no one vested enough in her wellbeing. And trust me, with her in jail, there isn't going to be a legion trooping for her release. Right now, I'm the only 'masses' she can count on to advocate for her freedom. I'm the closest thing to the toyi-toying, slogan-chanting public she could be assured would be at the police station demanding her release. Only, toyi-toying won't do it this time, money will, bail money to be precise. So, I have to find a gig. Not just any gig, a mega gig, and I have to find it really quickly.

The time I've spent entwasweni with Gogo Shezi, my gobela, has taken me out of circulation. So much so that I'm at loss about where to begin. She insisted that because I'm so close to ukuphothula, I stop with these other ways of divination I had been toying with and take time off work to prepare for umgidi wokugeza idlozi. So I took two months unpaid leave from work, with the condition that I could go in when they needed me and get paid for just those days. Which they haven't, which means that I haven't been paid for two months and I'm dead broke.

There is only one of two ways I could get my hands on some quick cash. One, I could call Lwazi and see if he would let me do one of his client's books. He has let me help him in the past, but only when he was involved in the entire process. I'd prepare the books, he would review and sign them off, and all was done. Or I could call Karen and see if she couldn't get me in touch with one of her gullible friends who wanted their tealeaves read, or their aura cleansed, or something. She had also let me have some of her clients when she had more than she could handle or when she was just not up to working with a specific person, for whatever reason. As easy as the second option sounds, it will get me into untold trouble with Gogo Shezi, because of the promise I made her.

If I call Lwazi, I'm afraid he won't stop going on about how I'm wasting my life. To him, my calling is one of my many excuses to not finish what I started. Apart from Lwazi coming at me about the state of my life, I wonder if he would still be prepared to let someone with half an accounting degree they had promised to finish years ago peer into his clients' records. He made it very clear that he would let me have some clients, but only if I came back to him after I had finished my studies. I have a feeling he's not going to do me any favours.

You see, I was in the middle of completing my degree when I got the calling. If I had magical powers to influence the course of events in my life, I would have wished that it wasn't really me the ancestors meant to call. But it was. So, heed the call I did, dropping everything I was becoming good at in the process. Serves me right that I got the calling, because before I did, I had been dabbling in a number of new age divination practices under Karen's guidance. Not that any of it was part of my plan, but one afternoon on campus I met Karen, who offered to do a reading for me. I was drawn to her, I liked her, and it all seemed so innocuous. So I figured, why not? Karen had learned from her mother, as she told me, who herself had been trained like the clairvoyants who followed the ways of Gaia.

Once she had aligned my chakras, balanced my energies and cleansed my aura, she told me – just like others before her – that I had psychic abilities. But, still, I didn't believe her. It wasn't until the telltale signs of me having a calling manifested that I started taking notice and thinking that maybe there was some truth to what people had been telling me all along. There was a time when, for such a young age and for the amount of money I was earning, I couldn't stay on top of my finances. Within the space of a year I had lost everything I had: I had lost my car and been kicked out of my flat. To top it off, I had failed every module I took that year, despite being dead certain that I had done well in the exams. I had damn near lost my mind. Then there were countless instances of déjà vu and the vivid dreams. Especially dreams of the ocean, which many swore was the definitive sign. Still, I wasn't convinced. Nevertheless, to stop Karen talking, I opened myself up to letting her teach me everything she knew about divination. I was open to this as long as it meant I wouldn't have to thwasa.

Karen took me under her wing and taught me all the basics of tarot reading, and numerology, by far my favourite. To see numbers transform to give meaning where there was just chaos was something I could never stop marvelling at. She also taught me palm reading, aura reading and teomancy. Textbook stuff, really. Things I practised only with my friends as party tricks. To break the ice at the same-same dinner parties I found myself invited to, when the night got to the point where it demanded entertainment.

On one or two occasions I really got into it and felt as if something real had happened. For example, there was this woman whose tealeaves I read, who started crying and told me just how spot on I had been. I realised then that there was something going on. Whether that thing was my dexterity with Karen's ways, or whether it spoke to my calling, I couldn't immediately make out.

So, maybe if I call Karen she could get me in touch with one of her Melville artist friends, who to me seem to have more money than sense, and are prepared to try just about any batshit idea. As long as it makes them come across as spiritual rather than the consuming beasts they really are.

Grief is strange because it will have you doing things you never thought yourself capable of. Beyond its energy sapping nature that leaves you with just enough drive to steady yourself against the blizzard of pain and bitterness to survive each day as it comes, it leaves you with little resolve. And when the storm begins to take on a shape you are familiar with, one you can predict, even, you turn and face the wind and do what needs to be done.

I think I'll call Karen. Today, this fits in the realm of the doable. I scroll down my phone and find her number. For a moment, I hesitate. I haven't spoken to Karen in such a long time and I hate to be one of those friends who only calls when they need something. But Karen and I have this kind of friendship where even if we don't speak for months, when we finally do, it's as if no time has passed. I take a deep breath and press the call button.

'Well, Nkads, to what do we owe the pleasure of this call?' she says in her ever-chipper voice.

'Well, hey. It's been a long time, I know,' I say, trying to suppress my embarrassment.

'Damn right, it has been. What's up?' she says, trying to avoid the awkwardness.

'I need a favour, man. No, scratch that, I need a mother of a favour,' I say.

'Name it, and we'll see what we can do.' Karen always refers to herself in the plural.

'I need money, so I need a gig. My mom died and I don't

have money to bury her. What's more, KG has managed to fucking get herself arrested, so I need to bail her out too. I need a client, a reading or two to make enough to pay for these things,' I say, almost hyperventilating.

'Shoo, Nkads, I'm really sorry about your mom. Uhhmm … didn't you say you and KG were over? Why is it on you to bail her out?'

'It's complicated,' I say.

'It always is with you, isn't it? Shoo, sounds like you need big money then. Let's see what we can do and we'll get back to you in a week or so. Tell you what, let's have drinks …'

'Karen, I don't have a week,' I interrupt her. 'I need this money as in yesterday. Besides, you know I don't drink anymore with my training,' I say.

'Sorry, honey, we forgot about that. Give us a day, two at the most, and we'll see what we come up with, yes?' she says.

'Thanks, honey. You're a life saver,' I say and hang up.

Day one goes by and Karen doesn't call. I'll be in the real dwang if she doesn't call. Day two goes by and I've just about bitten off the nails on all my fingers. *Please God let her call.* At 4.30 p.m. as I'm about to give up all hope, Karen calls. *She had better come through. Universe and all my ancestors in the ether and in the sea, she had better come through.*

The devil is a liar because Karen comes through. Like a slayer on Pegasus she comes through and lands me the mega gig of my prayers. This client is not the regular artsy type or the bored housewife; it's a business. A business looking to have its aura cleansed.

How bizarre I think, but *how fucking lucky can I get? I get to ply both my trades!*

'Need their aura cleansed,' is what they say, 'Need sound financial advice' is what I hear, but who am I to say what people need when they are explicit about it. If I can't read their Tarot, I'll just have to settle for reading their balance sheet and see if that doesn't score me a bigger cheque in the end.

Karen tells me I am to meet two women, Thabiso and Thandeka, who together go by the name Lesiba Communications. We are to meet at 12.30 p.m. at their offices in Parkhurst, on Wednesday. God, getting to Parkhurst is such a mission, but thank the mighty stars for my moped. I'll zip myself in and out to be back in time to attend to the weekend's preparations.

Getting out of the house will require weaving a watertight story or else I'm going to get into some deep shit with Gogo Shezi. If she finds out that I'm abandoning the weekend's preparations to hustle in ways she has specifically asked me not to, there will be some hell to pay. But, maybe, if I play my cards well I can get away with it. I'll tell her I'm needed at work. She said she would let me go if I was ever needed. My going to work pays the bills; even a gobela appreciates that. Also, she must understand if I need a little time out, these are fraught times; my mom has just died and my ex is in jail. My world as I know it has come to an end.

The story about Thabiso, the chief operations officer, and Thandeka, the general manager of marketing, as Karen told me, is that ten years ago, fresh out of university and after getting their postgraduate degrees, they set up this advertising agency. The two of them ran it for seven years with considerable success, until three years ago when they appointed Tom as their accountant.

Tom, who as people say, they didn't know from a bar of soap, was the sole custodian of their finances while they focused on growing the business. In addition to running the business they were both yogis who, as part of the perks they provided their staff, gave free yoga and Reiki sessions, all in the name of 'overall wellness'.

Lesiba Communications, which had done things in exactly the same way as it had for seven years, was now, for reasons they could not put their finger on, performing badly. So badly, in fact, that they even had to lay off some of their staff.

Above a bad set of books, the thing that concerned Thabiso the most was, 'The possibility of earning bad karma by bringing suffering to the lives of people we had willed to come and work for us,' as she put it when I met them.

'Damn! This kind of shit can't happen now, not today of all days. Not when I need to be in top form. This is not the day for things not to work,' I say as I kick start my moped for the fifth time.

God, I am so not in the mood for taxis. I would have to take three to get to Parkhurst from Phomolong. I am not in the mood to smell some umageza empompini who took a bath at a tap outside some ramshackle house. I am not in the mood to have my shoulder dug into by some woman's long nails in her bid to get the fare from the back seat to the driver. I am certainly not in the mood to sit so close to anyone that I feel as if they are about to share some deep secret about overthrowing the government or some such. I am just not in the mood for any of it. Today, I have to be in top form. My life depends on it.

People are strange. They are never sold unless there are

theatrics and paraphernalia involved, so I had better put on the performance of my life today. I need to carry all my charms to come across as the real thing and I can't psyche myself up in a taxi.

A couple more kick-starts and it comes alive, my jalopy. I am saved from the curse that is our public transport system. I zip my way around town and make it to the meeting twenty minutes early; this is a first for me, I am usually unforgivably late. When I get there, I realise I don't know which floor I should go to. I sit on the steps leading to the office block and finish a game of sudoku that I've been playing since the night before, another thing Gogo Shezi wouldn't be too chuffed about.

'You and that numbers game of yours,' she always complains.

I don't know what I imagined these two would look like when I meet them. In between all the things that have led up to this moment, I guess I've had very little time to imagine anything.

Thabiso is an out and out hipster. A hippy, even: torn skinny jeans, oversized shirt, bangles on both arms, vintage suede jacket, dreadlocks to her shoulders, and swathed in patchouli, all of this framed in a plus sized model's figure. Thandeka is Thabiso's stylistic inverse: Brazilian weave, manicured nails, chic wardrobe, expensive perfume you can smell from 10 kilometres away, impeccable make up, svelte, tall as a giraffe, and a slight twang that suggests she might have spent some time – but not too much – in the US.

I quickly take a liking to Thabiso because I think she has something of a sense of humour, albeit a dry one. I pick this up when we're in the office's kitchen after we've been introduced.

We're making herbal tea when I realise that I've emptied the last of the boiling water into my cup and say, 'Sorry for finishing all your water.'

'No worries,' she says, 'it's communal water. At least we can count ourselves lucky for having some. Things could be different.'

How very hippy, I think.

Thandeka doesn't warm up to me straight away. This has me thinking that this whole thing must be Thabiso's idea. No matter, I'm here now and I have to impress. There is so much at stake.

We sit down in their boardroom and I put on my cape with a cross on the back. I sprinkle some snuff on the surface of the table and the floor and light two candles – one for each of them. I burn some sage, never imphepho. I burn imphepho only at Gogo Shezi's; it always leaves me feeling out of sorts.

I tell them a little about myself and what I think I can do for them and then I ask them to tell me about themselves and the company. I leave out the fact that Karen has already filled me in a little on that. I also leave out the fact that I am an accountant in training. I tell them about some of the readings I've done for others and about ukuthwasa, and they seem intrigued. I think, to them, this makes me seem diverse enough to do a thorough reading that will cover a range of bases to restore balance to their business.

I've already decided that I'll go through my regular routine: I'll ask them to ask the question they want answered and in addition, I'll ask them to give me something material associated with the reading that they want done, so I can read that item and determine what intervention to provide.

They ask the question, 'Why is the business suddenly not

doing as well as it was in the past?'

A broad question, but fair enough.

They hand over a copy of their latest financial statements and I place my hand on it while closing my eyes to pick up its energy – theatrics, really. I ask if I can take a look at the financials and they agree.

I steal a quick glance at the major numbers; in other words, I do a quick horizontal analysis in my head. I'm good at this. You can place any set of financial statements in front of me, and immediately, I'll be able to spot the inconsistencies. It's just a gift I have. One I am happier to live with, unlike the one I had to accept.

Year on year, I see, their debtors have increased, a good or bad thing, depending. Their payroll costs have increased too. I also notice that their entertainment expenses have skyrocketed. This could either mean that they must be entertaining more clients, or someone is using this budget line as their own personal kitty. Their income, on the other hand, has remained pretty much the same. This doesn't add up. I ask whether they had more clients in the current year or employed more staff. They say no. I ask if they have any clients who have not been paying as they should. They tell me that overall, and as far as they know, they've been collecting all their bills on time, with the exception of maybe one or two small clients. I ask how many staff members have an entertainment allowance and how this is handled. They tell me it's just the two of them and Tom who use the company's credit cards. I ask if they've been entertaining more clients than they've been securing business. Not any more than usual, they say.

I feel a tug I can't explain. Maybe I've entered a zone I shouldn't be entering. I ask for copies of the financial statements from when the business was doing well and they bring these as well. Out of deference to them I ask again whether I can take a look. I hope they think of this as me reading the energy of when things were good, when what I am really doing, is a broader analysis.

The numbers start to do a dance. I tell them about the tug I feel and that I might need to do a little more reading, asking them whether I can take the financials home for 'further ancestral and numerological guidance'. Without any hesitation, they give me a few copies. My gut tells me I'm looking at a classic case of embezzlement. Precisely who and how will take a little more digging to establish. The credit card statements are where I'd start looking if they'd grant me that kind of access. Later, perhaps, I can point them in that direction.

I ask how often they review the books, not just the financials but also the source documents. Their response tells me that they are the definitive targets for embezzlement and 'creative accounting'.

'Hardly, ever since Tom came along,' Thandeka says.

I tell them I'm picking up that they need to be more hands on with their finances; this is where the spirits are telling me it's all going wrong.

'You have left your kraal unattended for too long, and now the vultures are starting to circle in,' I say.

I add that as soon as this evening, they should analyse their books and see what they find. Thandeka gives me a quizzical look. I suggest that we meet in the morning to review their findings and for me to give them my detailed reading, followed by an office cleanse with all the staff present. As many interventions as I can offer, I figure, as much money I stand to make.

Without a second thought, Thabiso agrees. Thandeka asks why we have to include the entire staff.

I explain, 'It is no good cleansing just the head because the entire body has to be cleansed too.'

It takes a bit of convincing on my part and a bit of bidding from Thabiso's side, but we finally manage to win Thandeka over.

When I get back to Gogo Shezi's, I find I have to come up with a pretty good reason for switching on my laptop. As much as she's okay with letting me go to work when I need to, she doesn't like me doing work at her house. I tell her I'm working to a deadline for a meeting that is happening the following day, for which they need the numbers. It takes a bit of pleading, but she finally relents and I spend the whole night going over Lesiba's books.

I conduct as thorough a financial analysis as I can. A pattern begins to emerge: consistency for the first seven years, with changes in the last three years. This could mean anything, really. I need to have a look at the source documents, now more than ever. I make do with what I have and hope that with my prompting they'll be able to uncover more. I'm certain, however, from what I've found, that something has shifted the balance in their books in the last three years.

In the morning I call Thabiso to confirm the meeting. I'm running out of time. For this weekend to work I need to bail KG out by Thursday afternoon and pay the undertaker by Friday afternoon because they have already committed to doing the funeral, provided they've been paid by then. So I have to be paid as soon as possible.

Gogo Shezi has already been receiving the mourners

on my behalf, has already selected the cow and the coffin, and bought the vegetables. KG has already drafted the programme and obituary on toilet paper, the only paper she has access to. All that's left is for it to be typed and printed. Everything is in place; all that's missing is the money to set the dominoes in motion.

On Thursday at midday, sleep deprived, I meet up with Thabiso. Thandeka is a no show. I tell her what the numbers have told me and Thabiso tells me what she, too, has found. She tells me Thandeka's card had irregular transactions and that when she looked at their billing invoices she found that the company's banking details had been altered to a number that looked eerily like Thandeka's personal account, which she suspects is the account their debtors have been paying into. We both agree that Thandeka is the thorn that must be weeded out to restore balance.

We also agree that I should continue to do a cleansing of the company. Again, I burn sage, and using umshanelo, I sprinkle saltwater around the office. Once I'm done, I assure her that things should start looking up. She seems convinced; that's all I ask for.

I hand her my invoice and ask that she settle it as soon possible. She tells me that with the way things are, the soonest she can pay is Monday.

This is exactly the kind of bosh I was hoping wouldn't happen. Now I have to ask Gogo Shezi to loan me the funeral money. Knowing her, she's not going to loan me any bail money.

And that's exactly what happens, she loans me just enough for the funeral, not a cent more. She also promises to do the eulogy in KG's absence. My mother's passing can only serve

Gogo Shezi, because now we have to do amagobongo, which means I might have to stay with her a little longer than I had hoped.

As the week from hell draws to an end, it all comes together, I guess. I learn that I'm not as alone in the world as I thought I was. With the invaluable help I got from KG and the help of people I had not thought would show up for me, Gogo Shezi being one of them.

What's more, with the success of the work I have done for Lesiba – what with having used my accounting and divination skills to alert them to the cause of their difficulties – I may have just found myself a niche market. As soon as ngiphothula I am branding myself as a Corporate Spiritual Advisor.

It will have to be another weekend in jail for KG, but at least I can give my mother a proper send off.

BLACK WIDOW

Unlike most people he knew whose biggest fear was death, his greatest dread was old age. And to be living it was pain enough. So the last thing he needed in this period of abatement was anything that would send him traipsing the dark alleys of memory. However, knowing full well as he did that life seldom delivered anyone's wishes to their exact specifications, when the moment called for him to walk down one such path, he rose to that occasion. But not without trepidation.

Ou-diePinkies was the sort of old man who, in his youth, had managed to squeeze in enough living in the hope that old age would find him spent and ready to surrender. A privilege denied him by life's whims and his inherited genes. Up until that day, when memory came knocking on his heart, he had spent most of his twilight years working at mending the holes on the soles of other people's shoes. This, in order to detract from the gaping hole in his own heart, which had first appeared on the day Afsar walked out on him, a little over half a lifetime ago. However, as much of a drudgery as his life seemed, he had somehow succeeded in finding a measure of peace. A peace which was disturbed by the arrival of the telegram, delivered by that thirsty postman who – despite Ou-diePinkies' house being the most marked in all of Phomolong – had managed to miss it at least three times and worked up an almost inextinguishable thirst before he eventually found it.

There stood two signs outside Ou-diePinkies' house. Both of which boldly declared, in different colours at that, that that spot of the world was called PINKIE'S COBBLER. Yet somehow, the postman had still managed to miss both the signs and the house.

But the postman's mistake was not unique to him and, as such, could not be attributed to any lack in his mental fortitude. Ou-diePinkies knew that when asked, 'Where's Pinkie's Cobbler?' very few of his neighbours would be able to point it out. Because over the years, mediated by their abundant wisdom, most of them had decided to ignore the assertions of the two signs and chose rather to call his house 'Pinkie's Cobra.'

The postman found Ou-diePinkies sitting on the veranda, scraping off the remains of a spider he had just killed from the heel of one of his customers' shoes. It had been a while since he had had occasion to receive a postman or any news in his house. The arrival of this one, which was preceded by two omens, triggered a feeling of dread within him. As the postman opened the gate in the manner of death's messenger, Ou-diePinkies remembered his dream from two nights ago. In this dream he had found a sack of spider eggs lodged under his bed. Connecting the invisible dots in his head, he wondered if the spider he had just killed was not the same one from his dream.

Once they were face to face the postman spat out a parched 'Good afternoon.'

Ou-diePinkies responded with a trembling one as his instincts now confirmed that whatever news the postman was bringing, he was not ready to receive. The exchange between the two men was as sparse as the message in the telegram.

'It is always the urgent news they send by telegram, isn't it?' he said, trying to shift the silence that stood between them.

'I'm afraid it is,' the postman replied, then licked his lips and swallowed as hard as he could what liquid there was still in his mouth. But realising that no amount of swallowing was going to quell his thirst, he spoke again and said, 'Brother, can I please bother you for a drink of water?'

Ou-diePinkies was about to rip open the envelope in his hands when these words made contact with his ears. On hearing them he tried to shake off the suspicion that this request was a ploy on the postman's part to have him delay opening the envelope until after he had left. He wondered if the postman already knew the contents of the telegram.

Why else would he ask for a glass of water just when I was about to open the envelope? He must know, Ou-diePinkies concluded.

'Not a bother at all,' he said as he stood to get the postman a glass of water. 'I have a feeling I too will need a drink once I have read whatever is in this note,' he muttered to himself as he disappeared into the darkness of his house.

In his absence the postman found a spot in the shade and perched on an up-turned bucket, not realising that suspended on the rusted gutter above that spot hung a black widow's web, only this one had no eggs in it.

In the kitchen Ou-DiePinkies' mind drowned in the flood of the many telegrams he had to read for his grandmother in his youth. A handful announcing 'So and so's son's marriage to so and so's daughter,'; a number proclaiming that 'so and so's daughter has given birth to her first child,' and the innumerable inevitably declaring 'the death of yet another so and so'.

When he resurfaced from the house with a glass of water in each hand, he gave one to the postman, and still holding the other, returned to his seat to continue the task of releasing the note from the envelope.

'It's the sort that is life changing, isn't it?' he said to the wind, as he ripped the envelope open.

With water in his mouth, the postman, although he was not the wind, nodded in response. Even men need company when faced with the arrival of unexpected news.

The note was brief in the manner of telegrams, and said as much in what was printed, as it did in what was not. It read:

AFSAR AKHALWAYA DIED 23rd FEBRUARY. WILL BE BURIED 25th FEBRUARY IN DURBAN. SEND SHOE SHE'S TO BE BURIED IN. DR CHETTY.

For a moment his senses left him. His body temperature dropped. His world shrunk. The hole in his heart widened. He knew the time had come for him to mend the one pair of shoes he had hoped his own death would save him from having to. Afsar's shoes. The pair she had worn out when theirs was still a path they walked together. There was no questioning it; the news of Afsar's passing had jostled him out of his somnambulist existence. Standing on the other side of awake he found that there were shoes to be fixed, a train ticket to be bought, a journey to be undertaken, memories to be laid to rest and, if good fortune favoured him, a modicum of life to be lived afterwards. With the cobwebs removed from his eyes it dawned on him why the telegram had made mention of only one shoe. Afsar, when he last saw her, was connected to the earth by only one leg. But which, the right or the left? This detail his mind withheld from him.

No matter this detail, there were still shoes to be found.

As soon as the postman left, Ou-diePinkies began rummaging through old boxes that had been stowed away for years either under his bed or on top of his wardrobe: inside which were things he'd hoped death would spare him the trouble of ever having to interact with. In one of the boxes he found only residues of mothballs. In another he found the black widow's egg sack of his dream and wondered whether he should, as he had in his dream, squash it or in light of the telegram, leave it be. He decided on the latter. He eventually found Afsar's shoes in the last but one box he looked in.

The pair of Florsheims, about which Afsar had once said '… it is the only pair I want to spend all of eternity in.'

Holding a hammer in one hand, Afsar's shoe in the other, and thoughts of him on his mind, Ou-DiePienkies started feeling like someone accosted by the memory of snakebite. This, however, did not stop him from putting in the work required to close the hole on the left shoe, and replace the heels on both. The luxury of leaving anything to chance was something he could not afford, even though he knew that half his labour was in vain.

It's astounding, the things that erupt in the mind. Especially at the point where memory brushes against anticipation, he found himself thinking, as he put the last nail on the left heel. He felt himself weighed down by the clamour of thoughts he had convinced himself his mind had long erased. Even in the spaces where it did not say, the telegram had made it clear: he had to get on the train, he had to face his demons, and he had to put the past to rest. But first, there was a ticket to be bought.

'Return Durban,' he said into the round hole on the stationmaster's window, as he pushed a few notes through the half-moon circle on the counter.

This was not his first excursion to Durban. There had been the first time, a year after the disintegration of their relationship when he had followed this same route. Waiting at the platform for the train's arrival, he played back remembrances of this first trip. Although the gravity which attended that journey – whose mission was to find and win Afsar back, in whatever state she was in – paled in comparison to the one attending this one, he still could not help but sink into its snare.

The easiest part of the first trip had been preparing for it. All he had to do then was dust out of obscurity his trusted outfit: the same one he was wearing even now, his chocolate brown tweed suit, white pin-stripe shirt, yellow tie, brown Stetson and tan Florsheims. He had already thought through, arranged, and armed himself with the explanations and supplications he was going to offer in the service of his task of winning Afsar over. In his mind's eye he could see it, how at the end of their talk Afsar would acquiesce to them starting anew and working towards building a life somewhat different from the one that had led to their separation. It was all sorted, or so he thought. Some people's hearts, Afsar's in particular, he remembered, had a way of preserving past events such that when revisited it seemed as if they had just happened.

It was at the Golden Mile that he found Afsar at the end of that first voyage. Upon enquiry, he had been informed that that was where he was most likely to find her. On seeing Afsar again after such a long time, Ou-diePinkies was struck, as he always had been by the smile on his, or more aptly her face, than by the vision of her as a rickshawala. Face-to-face with the man who had once enthralled him, and the woman she had now become, Ou-diePinkies felt himself at a loss for words. He stood back to take her in, item by item.

On her adornment, he read the entire story of their life together and hoped that no one else had been able to decipher it. Woven into Afsar's headgear Ou-diePinkies saw the shape of the house they had shared. On her earrings, he saw drawn in pink and blue a silhouette of the two signs that stood outside his house. On her black apron he saw a medley of buttons and mirrors arranged in the shape of an hourglass, each side containing an equal amount of sand, as if to mark the time of their parting. Their paths had diverged at a time when there was as much life ahead of them as there had been behind. Afsar was 35, and Ou-diePinkies, 32.

He took in her biceps, which although they had softened in the process of her becoming a woman, still spoke of her strength. He was held spellbound by the medley of colours on the wheels of her cart, a yarn of their past joys and pains. He saw for the first time her missing leg, and the stump that now stood in its place. He saw painted on the stump a bevy of black widows. On her other leg, underneath the white sock that reached her knee, he traced the sinew of her calf muscle. He fell in love again with the man of his dreams, who was now the woman of someone else's.

Through the crack on the tile she was standing on, he sensed the earth release a sigh. He envied its ability to do with no words what it would take him a million and still fail to express. But there was something of the future in the mehndi that decorated Afsar's hands, which confirmed the rumours that she had recently gotten married. It came as no surprise because women and marriage had been some of the things that wedged the rift between them, resulting in their split. Even though Ou-diePinkies could still not quite figure out why Afsar had decided to leave the world before him, he began to unravel the reasons she had left him the first time around.

'Oh! What a web we weave when at first we lie. Mostly to ourselves.' His grandmother's words rang in his ears.

When they were still together, Afsar and Ou-diePinkies – more on Ou-diePinkies' part than on Afsar's though – the lies took on a life of their own once they had started. The more these lies mutated, the more Ou-diePinkies found himself watching with a level of helplessness, as though he had no hand in their making. He watched as the first lie gave birth to the next, and the next to another, and another to another still. Until, at the end of all these lies was a child. His child. Borne of curiosa and a woman he had taken to seeing in order to feed his unspoken curiosity about women. Although he knew with the conviction of things unseen that he loved men: that he loved their bodies, that he loved the hair that grew on their faces, that he loved their touch, both gentle and strong. The ways of women and the world they inhabited also held a certain intrigue for him. There was a part of him that had always wanted to enter this world, to examine it, in order to know it, this world, which for him only existed in the realm of the imagination. He had always thought that growing up without any women in his life, except his grandmother, had robbed him of any chance of knowing the ways of women, and this he wanted to know. And this lack, he surmised, denied him the kind of intimacy he imagined was possible only with women. An intimacy he concluded not even Afsar was capable of giving him, so that the combination of his wonder and imagination intensified his yearning for a relationship with a woman. But how to go about it, he had no idea. And not knowing any other way he followed the ways of men, and dismounting curiosa's bed, he found himself holding curiosity's child.

It wasn't so much the resultant child that enraged Afsar, as much as the lies and secrets surrounding it, that left her feeling spurned. The birth of Ou-diePinkies' child deepened Afsar's feeling of lack and illuminated her inability to give Ou-diePinkies the one thing she did not have in her to give. Afsar, who had felt herself more of a woman her entire life than she had let on, not just to Ou-diePinkies but to the world, felt aggrieved. Just because she did not look it, or act it, or insist on it, or smell it, it did not take away from the fact that she felt it deeply every single day, in silence and in the crevices of her soul. This is why, perhaps for Afsar, the birth of Ou-diePinkies' child presented as one of the steepest obstacles she felt they would have to surmount. This because she felt, and justifiably so, that they had spent themselves overcoming so many others in the past.

In the aftermath of the lies and dejection Afsar began to feel as if the wind had been pulled from beneath her sails. She 'could no longer live like that,' she told Ou-diePinkies, in no uncertain terms. She needed to set herself free and fly, embrace her being in its entirety, and begin to express herself like the free spirit she really was but had kept bottled up even at the time they first met. Ou-diePinkies concurred, but not without any pain.

From the moment the child was born, Afsar, for the first time, felt liberated to let surface the parts of herself that she had kept subjugated all her life. She reckoned the time had come for her to tear down all the walls she had built around herself and announce, not only to Ou-diePinkies and the world, but to herself as well, that she was every much the woman her own heart had been hankering for.

And so, she took the first step in the journey, at the end of which she hoped to encounter herself. In pursuit of this, she dusted out of the crevices of her life every scrap of material she had secretly been gathering that would guide her to the place of her heart's hankering. With all the tenacity in her being she pored over every newspaper article, every magazine clipping, every excerpt from a book she had kept, and read and read and read about how she could make it so that she was a she.

There were the newspaper clippings containing the stories of Christine Jorgensen, and April Ashley, the most well-known people to have received gender reassignment surgery, which she had kept and which kindled her determination. But still, she doubted herself. She allowed a naysaying voice to live inside her head, occasionally reminding her of the nigh impossibility of her desire. This despite the fact that there also lived a resolute certainty in her mind of how badly she wanted to realise her wish. The realist in her told her that even if she were somehow able to triumph over the very glaring reality of her financial inadequacy there would still be the emotional crags that she would have to prevail. She wondered whether she had it in her to let slide the jibes she knew would attend her, just like they attended Jorgensen: about how she had been the only man to have gone 'abroad to come back a broad'. Or whether she would be able to survive it, were it to happen to her as it happened to Ashley that one of her friends were to out her as transgender and cause her embarrassment. As unnerving as these prospects were, she soldiered on. In fact, so desperate was she at some point that she even considered joining the army, just so she could get a state subsidised transition. But this was a time in history when there was no place for Indians in the military. But still, she kept trying. With every failed attempt the distance between Afsar and Ou-diePinkies grew bigger and bigger and slowly, they began to drift apart. Afsar's despondency had led her to a place where she was almost about to resign herself to defeat, when news of a doctor who could help came. She received the news with the jubilation of a people who receive the rains after a protracted drought. The news, however, came as a mixed blessing. The blessed side being that at no financial cost to her, but at great risk, Afsar could present herself as a subject for medical trials that were still at an early testing phase but which, if successful, would yield the desired result. The doctor responsible for these tests was only just beginning to test his techniques, but those in the know said that he had made great strides and could be trusted. Afsar signed herself up as a volunteer and took a big leap on her journey. Said doctor was based in Durban, which meant that this would be the road that Afsar would have to travel in order to become the woman of her dreams. Throughout all this, Ou-diePinkies had not counted on the one thing he loved most about Afsar – her untethered spirit – becoming the same thing that would fuel his resentment of her. The cursed side of the blessing was that the end of the reassignment surgery marked the beginning of a love affair between Afsar and the man who had finally managed to make her the person she always knew she was. So that when Dr Chetty proposed to Afsar after a few months of courtship, she did not hesitate. They were married. And so it was that Afsar bolted out of Pinkies' heart, leaving a gaping hole in it.

The whistle announcing the arrival of the train pulled Ou-diePinkies out of his reveries and brought him back to the platform. As soon as the train stopped, he picked up his bags, got on board and looked for a place to sit. He found an empty compartment, walked inside it, stowed his bags, closed the door behind him, and soon realised that unlike the present, the door to the past, once opened, was not as easy to close.

The train pulled off, marking the beginning of a journey that would darn the distance between his past and future. In between the kuchung-kuchung of the train, the sound of the wind, and the landscapes that fleeted past the window of his compartment, he felt himself transported to the place of their first meeting. It was Kwa Sis Getty that they had met, one of those shebeens that lined the then burgeoning Johannesburg Gold Reef. Even then, Ou-diePinkies had sensed that a hand much stronger than fate had orchestrated the crossing of their paths. He thought of it as something that had been ordained.

It's the smell, always, that gets you when you go to places like these for the first time, he thought. *It's an odd smell: a combination of human flesh in its most natural state, covered by the scent of cheap perfume and yearning. It's the smell of dances both recently and long performed, and the waft they leave floating in the air in the aftermath. It's the smell of the present and the past clinging onto the walls, graffiti style, as if to say, 'so and so was here.' Only, unlike graffiti, the names of those 'so and so's' are secrets that the walls keep to themselves,* he mused. *It's the smell of raw need. No, it is the smell of desire fulfilled and thwarted. Only the nose knows, and after a while only it can distinguish between the smells of those who are still there and those who have long gone.*

Afsar. She smelled different. Her smell was a blend of hope, Old Spice and optimism. A smell known only to a handful of people who she had allowed to get close enough to get to know her, and in time were able to distinguish it from the fog of the dominant one. Ou-diePinkies was one of those people. In addition to the smell, the other memorable thing about these places was the assortment of colourful personages they attracted. He remembered how, on his first visit to Kwa Sis Getty, he had to navigate a sea of faces in order to end up standing nose-to-nose with Afsar. He recalled how he had to steer his course around the woman who, with the help of makeup and pencil, had managed to overdo on her face what Gerald Sekoto was beginning to perfect with subtlety on canvas. He recalled how he had to meander beyond the drunken brute who, in spite of warning anyone within earshot 'not to trust anyone who calls you my friend', himself went on calling everyone 'my friend'. Past the man with the fat fingers, whose mind seemed to have been occupied with the task of reconciling his level of drunkenness to the empty pay packet in his pocket. And behind these faces and many others, there she was, Afsar. The man who, at first sight, caused such an effusion of passion inside him. He remembered how he had felt a rapture invoked by a mix of anxiety and desire. He recalled how he had to take a deep breath to compose himself in the face of imminent transgression. Theirs was a desire that would break a number of heavenly and earthly laws in order for it to be fulfilled.

There was the prophetess's foretelling, which at the time did not make much sense, but which he thought needed considering.

The prophetess had said, 'There will be many obstacles to overcome when you finally meet the one who will claim your heart. At your first meeting, he will appear as one thing, but when the time comes for your paths to separate, he will have become another.'

She had been cryptic in the way of prophets, but she had been right about the obstacles. In the material world, only a few steps stood between them and the imagined act hinted at by the meeting of their eyes. In the world of the law stood a number, constructed specifically to restrict their contact. The hue of their skins, the sameness of their sex, the stark difference in their way of life and the landscape of their worlds, all of which had been arranged to stop them from touching. Yet, despite these obstructions, they found a way to touch each other from that evening on. But not without difficulty.

In the spaces between the train's whistle at every station, he heard again the penny whistle of their Sunday morning music. In the tremble of coaches, he heard the drums of their shared favourite songs. In the shuffle of his fellow passengers' feet and their late night snores, he heard the percussions Afsar had played. And in the silence of the night interrupted by the song of crickets, he heard the melancholy of the lyrics that accompanied the songs Afsar sang.

Ou-diePinkies was thinking about the sort of inscription they would put on Afsar's gravestone, 'HERE LIETH A WHOLE PERSON WHO LIVED A FULL LIFE', when his thoughts were interrupted by the ticket examiner's knock. He opened the door, fished his ticket from the inner pocket of his jacket, and handed it to the ticket examiner for clipping. When he took his ticket back, he noticed the ticket examiner's shoes: the same as Afsar's. His thoughts transported him back to the day when Afsar's pair was bought. Afsar loved her Florsheims for what their makers said about them: a 'combination of style, comfort and high quality'. Attributes which could just as easily have been used to describe her. This is why it had not bothered her much that just this one pair would cost her a whole month's salary; she had to buy them for her thirtieth birthday. Afsar wore those shoes, and only those, until the day she walked out of Ou-diePinkies' life. And even then, only because they needed mending.

As the train pulled to a halt he knew that he had come as close as he ever would to arriving. At the end of this journey, with the not so distant future and the past knitted into the web of his thoughts, there was no denying it any longer. Afsar was no more. She had done her part. She had lived the exact number of years allotted every person – seventy, not a day more, not a day less. It finally dawned on Ou-diePinkies, that from that point on, there would no longer be any arms of hers to yearn for, any lost legs to suppress, or any unfulfilled desires to cling to. All that remained was the hope that both the man and woman she had been would finally find a comfortable resting place in the shoes of her choosing.

Life has a strange way, he thought as the Durban sign came into view, *of returning you to places where you've once been, if only to deliver you to its desired destination. Ashes to ashes, dust to dust*, the statement resounded in his head as he disembarked his train of thought. Inside his compartment he gathered himself, doffed his hat, and sensed a new realisation sink through the pores of his 68-year-old conscience.

Despite everything that had happened, he came to accept that the present and what little of it there was now left, was the only place for him to live. The past and the future lived in another time.

Jocasta's Hairballs

Anna

Too much has been said about love children by people who know plenty little about both love and children. My father and mother, too, when they were talking about having me, could have easily fit into this category. I heard them speak about this idea of spurious offspring in falsettos liberated from the imprisoning confines of their pearly whites, while concealing from each other the sound of their dripping hearts and I knew right then that they were making a big mistake. But so consumed were they by the notion of a love child that they did not even question that I had to be conceived three times before I finally conceded to being born.

The first time I was conceived … well, unhappiness is the word that comes to mind because, suddenly, they had it in abundance.

My father carried his behind the fermenting stench of alcohol breath and a heart tainted with regret. Regret. Now, of all the feelings he had let creep into his heart, regret was the one he was most familiar with.

My mother bore her share secretly and had perfected the art of neatly stacking most of it, the bits that she did not swallow, at the back of her throat.

In their not so conjugal bed, my father laid his head on a pillow of disenchantment. The same pillow he had deliberately decided to deprive of the displeasure of his tears. Choosing, rather, to shed them on the bosoms of countless other women, his virtual harem. There was something he found soothing in shedding tears on pillows that had sampled a large enough variety, so much so that they made no fuss about the taste of any new flavours.

My mother.

My mother spent most of her feigned sleep silently tossing and turning, trying to tame the pain of her violent loneliness, the brand known to visit the sort of women who have lain too long in beds long deserted by love.

For her reprieve, she busied herself with the business of looking good and making everything around her look good. Theirs was not a modest life, not by any stretch of even the most inelastic imagination.

My father's compunctions were countless and most of them dated back to when he himself was still a foetus. The biggest and primary resident of his mind when I was first conceived concerned the vow which, no matter how hard pressed he felt to make it, he could not bring himself to. 'Til death do us part,' he could not bring himself to say to my mother, no matter how hard my grandmother pressed him to. No matter how he had already vowed in the seclusion of his heart – where no cows had to be slaughtered, or beer brewed, or priests bribed to officiate, or particular guests present to be amused – that he would never live apart from the woman who would bear him his first child. Part of resisting this vow was the fear that if he made it, knowing himself as he did, he could trust himself to find a way to make breaking the vow a self-fulfilling prophecy.

There is a sombreness I sense lives in the vows that people make in the presence of those they can see with the naked eye, and those who live in worlds where bodies are not a necessary accessory for life. Graver, still, I discern, are the vows that people make in the presence of their souls as sole witness. My father had made a myriad of vows and broken a limitless amount at will. However, this one, he could not bring himself to make.

There is a deep yearning, which I came to grips with only when I was finally born. A realisation that children who have swung too long from the branches of broken family trees hold in the stems of their beings, the desire to raise their offspring under conditions markedly different from their own. One of my father's most pressing determinations was to give me the one thing that he himself never had: a tree with all its branches intact. That wasn't until his familiarity with broken branches stirred in him a violent desire to chop up, as if for firewood, the very tree that he had once diligently laboured at keeping whole.

It was the unhappiness and countless regrets which, in the measures they saturated his entire being, contaminated every word that came out of his mouth and made my mother's life a waking nightmare.

Souls unencumbered by flesh and bones have an immense capacity for compassion. So, in my compassionate form, I decided to release both my parents, but my father particularly, from the yoke of their unhappiness. Hoping that, freed from the burden of having to contend with me, he would be absolved from the spectre of his misery. I decided that I was not going to stay for a full term in my mother's womb.

Now that I think of it, it's frightening just how spontaneous my decision was, and maybe a little cruel, too. I realise now that I did not think it through. I made and executed my decision when my mother went in for the sixth visit to her gynaecologist. While she struggled to find parking, it hit me there and then, this compassion. It was in a flash that I did it. It couldn't have been longer than a split second and what needed to be done was done. It seemed to make sense at the time, and in my still-forming heart I concluded that it was for their benefit. It was, I remember, at the exact moment when my mother was about to find a parking spot that I performed the final manoeuvre: a swift turn to the right to position my neck in such a way that it would be strangled by the umbilical cord. Two split seconds of suffocation and one yet to be formed gasp released and I had expedited the earliest suicide ever.

By the time the necessary doctor's room congenialities had been exchanged, the ultrasound gel ordered and duly charged to her account, and she had changed into those sage green gowns, I was long gone. My mother, however, only realised this when, in place of the peep-peep sounds she had grown accustomed to during these visits, the ultrasound machine was silent.

My inexplicable death seemed to bring them closer, but only for a while.

The closeness lasted until they decided to have me again. This time, I must confess I did not even want to be conceived. My mother's body had been transformed into a haven of fear. I was afraid that if I allowed myself to cuddle up to it for all of nine months, I would be born as fearful. It wasn't malevolence disguised as sympathy this time around; it was the dread with which I had to share my mother's womb. It had blended with all the liquids that flowed through her body. It coursed through all her veins, danced unashamedly up and down her spine and filled her womb. She was afraid of everything, but most of all she was afraid of being so afraid.

With time, I reconsidered my fate and I imagined staying would help rid her of it. I thought myself an unborn exorcist. But there was nothing to it, I stayed with her. She carried me to term and she was able to make all the allocated visits to the doctor as expected of someone in her condition.

My father slipped back into his old ways and her fear solidified. He started treating her as if she did not exist and acknowledged her only when he willed or demanded it.

I died my second death on the day I was due for delivery. An eighteen-hour labour had me jostling with the doctor's forceps as he tried to pull me out through the wall of fear blocking my mother's uterus. There was a part of me then that so wanted to come out, but I felt myself constantly banging against this hedge of fear that Jo had allowed to coat her womb.

Third time's a charm, or so they say. I ran out of reasons to not let myself be born.

My mother had near given up hope that she would ever have children, and in conceiving me the third time, she was really just going through the motions. My grandmother wanted grandchildren as badly as most grandmothers do; my mother was being called names that mouths as small as mine should not have to repeat.

Her silence intensified.

She took to speaking only in her heart. It was only because I was privy to her inner ruminations that I knew she was ready to have me. In the depths of her heart, where no one heard her, she spoke of the uncontainable spring of love that flowed within her. She spoke of her frustrations, which none of the mortals surrounding her appreciated. She spoke of the sting caused by loving a man who so clearly did not want to be loved, not in the way she had proposed to love him, anyway. She spoke of her desire to frolic in these springs quenching anyone, everyone's thirsts. She spoke of the taste of the wounds, lodged at the back of her throat, which she hoped to throw up someday. The way cats do the hairballs gathered in the process of cleaning themselves.

It was when she cried during one of their conjugal obligations, that I knew I was ready to be born of this woman so transformed by time.

He engraved himself onto me. She made his seed shine and I let up the fight. It was time to be born. I let up a bit too soon, I think. I think my father secretly hoped that this time too, nothing would come of it.

On a Monday like any other, Jo came back from the hospital with the pink receiving blanket in her arms covering the me that would witness way too much in a short space of time.

On that same Monday, Vido came home bearing a bunch of roses for the woman who had borne his first child and felt himself again pulled down by the weight of his vows.

His mood grew. A level that was possibly far too taciturn than it usually was.

On the second day of my arrival, my mother received her first curse from him. Again, things that ears as small as mine should not have to hear. On our fifth day back, she got her first black eye. It was on the seventh that I knew my eyes had seen way more than anyone should see on the day the Lord rested.

I suspected that he would do that to her: slap her around, be bored every time she opened her mouth, be impatient when dinner was late or a degree or two colder. I had not anticipated that he would do to her what he did to her with his shoes.

JOCASTA

Love hurts my eyes every time I fall and I seem to fall a lot. Last night I fell again but, this time, not in love. I fell straight onto the pointiest point of his new pair of shoes, landing eye first. He had to let me see them that close, otherwise I would not have noticed them: the black and grey snake leather and hide shoe, box shaped with two pivotal points. A resplendent vision of the serpent and the beast in perfect accord, inside a box they did not choose for themselves.

I had just put Anna down in her cot and thought myself successful at convincing her to take a break from the weeping she started while still in my belly.

I went into the kitchen to fix myself a cup of tea. I warmed up the teacup and remembered MaEster telling me 'tea does not taste the same unless the cup it is drunk from is itself warm and ready to receive it'. I took the tea bag out of the container, another thing she would have admonished me for.

'Good tea must be brewed and allowed to trek, I don't trust these things of yours that cook in cups,' I could almost hear her saying. She was very sweet, MaEster, and set in her own ways too. Her only flaw was that she cared more for the aesthetics of things than she cared for the things themselves.

Two teaspoons of sugar, a dash of warm milk, and I thought I was ready to sit down and enjoy the silence that filled the room now that Anna was finally asleep. I leaned over the kitchen counter to take my first sip. Three of the tears that Anna had not cried came out my own eyes, landed in the centre of my teacup, and caused a small storm.

The milk curdled. The words POST PARTUM DEPRESSION embossed themselves on my mind, although I knew there had been a 'PRE'.

The front door opened. He walked in, dragging a split second behind him the aura of a solitary rotten lemon left in a fruit basket where all the sweet fruit had been eaten.

He let out a sullen hello. It landed straight in the receptacle in which I thought my fear of him had been buried since Anna was born, breaking it into a million and three shards. Today, he was at his most taciturn.

Because his condition was not new, over the years, I had developed a few stratagems to survive him. Vido. The man who had fallen in love with my tenderness only to insist on hardening me, because he thought I was too yielding.

At times like these, I found there were three knacks that worked for me. The first and most useful involved taming my screams so that they sunk to the bottom of my handbag, away from his ears and scrutiny. The second involved the skilful way in which I had trained my eyes to bleed silently onto our not so conjugal pillows, thirty minutes, always thirty minutes after the lights went off so as not to create any discomfort for him. Lastly, from cats, I had learned the grace of throwing up hairballs flavoured with my pain in private, away from his gaze. Felines do it in secrecy for the very reason that it is an unsightly thing to do, purging one's pain under the gaze of an uninterested audience.

To recompose myself and to turn off the buttons of fear I had felt switched on as soon as he walked in, I settled for small talk.

'How was your day?' I asked him casually.

In response, he let out a snort. 'What's for dinner?' he asked.

Yes, dinner.

At that moment I remembered that there was something I had forgotten to do today and until he asked, I hadn't been too sure what it was.

'Oh, I'm so sorry. I haven't made anything. But I can quickly make you some noodles, if that's okay?' I said.

He shot daggers at me and I felt the stab of the fear he meant to rouse.

He reached over, grabbed me by the scruff and barked directly into my ear, 'And this will bring the count to fourteen goddamned minutes of those hideous things you have been forcing me to eat ever since you came back from the hospital!' A tad loud for someone in his mood. 'Not even a dog would agree to being served this same goddamned shit, day in and day out! Have you lost your last ounce of respect for me?!'

He banged my head against the kitchen counter. The cup in my hands slid off and broke into a hundred pieces. I swallowed my screams.

He landed a backhand slap on my right cheek and I let my eyes swallow the tears. Then it happened. The chair moved from underneath me and he tried to pull me by my hair. He missed. I slid from the chair now giving way and landed eye first onto the pointiest point of his shoe, which had been readying itself to meet a part of my face in any case.

I think I swallowed all the hairballs at the back of my throat.

My defences were so low I knew I was dying. One can only take so many beatings without cracking under the strain. It was the fear that made it so easy for me to let go.

Anna woke up, I think, because the last sound I remember hearing was that of her waking cry. Thank God I had made an extra bottle for her. Vido had fed her once and I hoped he would know what to do now.

ESTER

It was the shatter I felt before the thud my ears actually heard, which raised that flag that always goes up at the back of my head every time something grave is about to happen. I ignored it, thinking that my mind was playing tricks on me. It often did.

Vido was my sister's son and I loved him as much as a mother is supposed to love her son. He came to stay with me soon after his mother died. He was seven at the time and had already committed six of the seven deadly sins. He had not gotten around to pride. In fact, throughout his life, he never got around to pride. He believed too much in his own insignificance to let himself sin that way. He did a pretty good job at all the others, though. Sloth was his favourite pastime, followed by anger, which he showed out of habit, then greed, which he could not get enough of. Lust, gluttony, and envy were still budding within him and I feared these would be the ones he would most excel at when he was older.

I often wondered what it was that Jo saw in Vido to stay with him as long as she did. He was very difficult to love, Vido. Maybe there was something in him that spoke to some or other thing in her. There is something about kids who have spent too much time swinging off branches of broken family trees that draws them to each other.

In the years they were together, fatigued by giving Vido the love he was so clearly unprepared to receive, I set about developing a relationship with Jo that reached deeper than the legal ties that bound us would ordinarily permit. Without realising, I had come to feel as if it was Jo, and not Vido, with whom I shared blood-knots. So, when I heard the thud, I should have prepared myself to unravel the ominous omens of a string of amens I kept hearing Jo saying in my head.

If memory serves me well – it's been misfiring these day so I don't rely on it much anymore – the shatter I sensed before any sound was that of her fear vessel breaking into a million and three shards.

At the time I thought nothing of it; I was crocheting booties for my first grandchild. There is nothing more satisfying for a grandmother than making things for offspring two generations from you. There is nothing that beats the feeling of being someone's progenitor. So I was engrossed in that until my attention was interrupted between the second last stitch and the start of a new row by the sound I had no doubt heard: the sound of Jo's skull landing on the kitchen floor.

I dropped my needles.

They pricked the earth at the exact moment Jo let out her last breath.

When I got to the kitchen, Vido was begrudgingly swallowing his fourteenth minute's serving of those noodles I had been warning Jo against.

'Food that cooks in a cup is not good for anyone,' I had

told her.

But would she listen? They never listen, the kids these days, living their instant existences.

Her blood was still fresh on his shoes, most of it at the pointiest point of his snake and beast marriage of a shoe. Some of it still oozed from her eye. A portion of it that could not come out from there forced open her ears and mouth to gush out, letting out the words she had been repeating silently in her heart. Pity, she had encrypted most of it so much I could not understand what she was saying. So no one had any idea what the last words to have come out her mouth were. Even in waking life, though, she never spoke much, that Jo. Ever since her second miscarriage, she swallowed up anything she thought worth saying.

I could swear I saw a blood-stained hairball hanging out of her mouth, but it could have been my mind playing with me again.

I knew the police's number but struggled to remember it. The shame of dirty laundry hanging for all to see paralysed me into a state of selective amnesia.

VIDO

Anyone who knew me well enough would have told you that I suffered from a condition that psychology was yet to diagnose – ASD, Attention Seeking Disorder. Like anyone with a pathology they are aware of I tried as best as I could to hide mine. Most times I failed. Especially when I felt I was denied the attention I deserved.

David spoke to me in that way that colleagues should not speak to each other, no less in the presence of their boss. For a man so small, he sure did a good job at stealing my thunder.

If you ask me, on that day, he was the one displaying ASD tendencies.

So he got it, that promotion I had been slaving for since I joined the company along with the recognition I had been trying to earn since I was seven. A sling, a monkey trick or two and he, not me, gets to become chief finance officer. He got the pat on the back that goes with it as well: the car big enough to house his Napoleonic ego. The women – well the women he's always had, thanks to his metrosexual inclinations. Women will buy anything cosmopolitan and Raphaelic enough to feed their gullible minds. Deep down – if only they knew – he held them with the same amount of contempt as we all did. Now, with his big title, he would not even have to exert himself by pretending to fall for their wiles. They would just be his for the taking.

And me, what did I get? A child that never stopped crying, a partner who felt it her obligation to join that same child every time she did, these bags under my eyes from slaving to get noticed, this knot in my stomach and my father's disappointed eyes staring at me into eternity. Fortune does not only favour fools, she does so because she herself is a bit of an idiot, I think, birds of the same feather.

And when I got home I was expected to deal with it all by myself, with no help, not even from my father who was now supposed to be this all seeing eye. All of this while the weeping willows did as they do.

Jocasta would just go on about her day as if it was the most interesting thing in the world. What was so fascinating about dirty diapers, the smell of baby spit, and the meaningless twitches that Anna made?

'Oh, she smiled today. Then she scratched her eyes, then this that, then that this.' Ooooh she went on and on and on and on.

We wasted way too much time interpreting meaningless gestures made by this child. Don't get me wrong, I love Anna too and all that, but I couldn't spend more than five minutes talking about what she did or did not do while moving her body, when there were much more interesting things to talk about.

And oooh, Jocasta's laziness! Man, her laziness just drove me round the bend! It was as if she did it just to spite me. In the last week since she had returned from the hospital, she had served up a cumulative twelve-minute serving of those stupid noodles that cook in a cup.

Here I was thinking my aunt Ester's dog vomit tasting soup, which she at least actually took the trouble of cooking for longer than two minutes, was the worst thing I had ever put in my mouth. Now, thinking about it, I'd soon have some of that than be subjected to yet another ludicrous serving of those two-minute things. I swore to God that if she ever gave me another helping there would be hell to pay. I would moer her so hard that everyone who went to the Beijing conference would sommer go back and burn their bras again. Strue's bob, I didn't care.

I walked into that baby-spit-smelling denizen of sorrow to see that face that had not smiled in eleven months. Instead of asking me kindly, like a good partner would, how my day was, she almost interrogated me.

'*How* was your day?' she asked in that Nandi voice.

Is that any way a man must be welcomed into his home? I'm sure Pastor Paul had a thing or two to say about that kind of behaviour. It was that stupid Nandi who had been influencing Jo with her heretic feminist thoughts. Feminist-nyeminist. Go burn your underwire bras, I say. No one comes into my house and says, 'women submitting to men is a silly old patriarchal ploy to keep women subjugated'. Silly old patriarchal ploy my foot! Those words came out of God's mouth Himself! What next? That God did not create the earth and we somehow evolved out of the sea?

Nothingpeevedmeoffmorethanthoseridiculouspseudo americanaccentspeakingvegandietpreferring meditatingmantrachantingincenseburningacademics and their propensity for making unfounded claims. Which, I might add, they always failed to substantiate without the use of their R50 worth polysyllable words. Because if you took away those mumbo-jumbo words they use that were meant to razzle-dazzle and dumbfound you, there was really little substance to what they had to say. I was yet to find that one scientist worth their American accent and R50 words, who could tell me, why, why, why, if they claimed as they did that we evolved from fish and chips, how come that cycle did not repeat itself today? Huh? Was there any academic out there in the poststructuralpostdoctoralpostmodernistposttoastiesp ostbox-postpoststratosphere worth their mettle, who could tell me just that one thing?

I lost it when I walked in through the door and could so clearly see that Jo had not so much as lifted a finger to try and make the house look a bit decent. I knew, just like that, that that stupid Nandi had been to visit. With her 'coochie-coochie-coo's what a cute baby' out the one corner of her mouth and her 'you should not let him treat you that way' out the other.

Her asinine ideas explained why she did not have a man to call her own, choosing rather to cavort with women. It explained, also, why Jo sat there sipping her tea with no dinner cooking on the stove, another of that obtuse Nandi's influences. I com-puh-lee-tly fuh-lipped, like I knew I would, when she said she had forgotten to make dinner and that we would be having another serving of those godforsaken two-minute noodles for the seventh day in a row! This time, seasoned with her tears, just to add a different flavour!

No man should have to live like this. So, I let her have it. I probably shouldn't have.

But I guess it's too late now to be feeling remorseful, what's done is done.

If I thought Anna had been weeping for no reason before, I could now congratulate myself for having successfully given her one.

There is something about children who are orphaned while they are still infants, which makes it impossible for them to find a comfortable place in the world to call their own. I guess it was the kick of the beast and the sting of the serpent that did the trick. I did not kick her any harder than I had in the past. Heck! In fact, I had kicked her harder on other occasions. I guess it was the shoes and the day's anger, which they had absorbed by the point they met her eye.

I so wanted to sob but could not bring myself to do it.

From where I sat I could see the blood oozing out of her eye, her ears and her mouth, but could not bring my mind to think what to do. Then something else came out of her mouth. A blood-stained hairball, I think, which stopped time and catapulted me into a yesterday I knew only too well. Only, in this yesterday, the woman whose head lay in the puddle of blood was not Jo but my mother.

Why had my mother come back from the dead only to die the same death she died 28 years ago, this time in my kitchen?

Anna started weeping, seconds after I took Jo's pulse and confirmed what I suspected. She was dead. One kick! One small kick in the eye and she died on me! How absurd, how very absurd!

Ma Ester walked in to find me trying to eat the poor excuse of a dinner Jo had offered me before she left. I couldn't help but be afraid that she would call the police and send me away, like I know she's been dying to since my mother died.

DELILAH

I thought I would finally emerge from my private hell as soon as Vido was completely mine. But now that he was, my descent into sorrow intensified. I took my first step into Hades when he walked in through the front door smelling like death. His eyes were bloodshot, his hands tremulous, his mood sombre. He carried a seriously mournful Anna on his back. He was shaking so much I thought he would drop her.

'She hasn't stopped crying since I left home. See if there is anything you can do to make her shut up,' he barked.

He had never brought her here before. This would have been a pleasant surprise, a sign that we were moving forward in our relationship, if only the smell of death did not hang so belligerently over him.

'Is everything okay?' I asked him.

'It's Jo,' he said. 'It's Jo and the things she drives me to do,' he repeated, this time letting out a big sigh.

The first of a million and three he would let out during our time living together.

'I didn't mean to, but hey, what's done is done,' he

mumbled under his alcohol tainted breath. I began to curse the hen that laid the golden egg in my shoes, forcing me to step into Jo's.

It took two days of him living in my house for me to realise that the moments that used to be our trysts would turn into tiffs that would turn into fists. If he had done that to Jo, what in nirvana's name made me think that ours would be a paradisiacal existence? More so now that he had firmly entrenched me in Jo's shoes by bringing Anna here.

On the third day, he finally told me.

'Jo is dead,' he said, rummaging for beer in my fridge, which did not hold men's milk. 'She made me do it,' he said nonchalantly as he banged the fridge door. 'You have no beer!' he let out shrilly, followed by one of the sighs I now kept count of.

Living with him, because it was clear he was not going back to his house any time soon, was like committing a protracted suicide. I really wished fortune, as I had thought it would be if he became completely mine, had not shown me her pearly whites.

Burst at the seams with angst is all I ever seemed to be able to do in those days. My own dread amplified daily and joined Jo's. He insisted on it. Every day I felt myself move closer to the rimless ridge of misery. My steps into Hades turned into a trot, then a gallop. Anywhere but here was where I wanted to be, so I sprinted further down.

In Hades, on Persephone's bosom, I set myself free. I let what he called my solitary mass hysteria loose through the cracks of my flimsy bliss. Up here on earth, Vido did not like that much.

I saw it in the ways he looked at me; it was no longer me he saw. Every day in his eyes I slowly turned into the Jo he had grown so irritated with because he thought her soft. I could see that if I stayed with him, it would only be a matter of time before he did to me what he had already done to her.

On the seventh day, I let go of all inhibition and the sorrow came tumbling out my eyes. No longer able to censor my tears I let myself nestle in the twin streams of torment, one for myself and the other for Jo. I lent my tear ducts to Jo, so that she could cry in his presence the tears she had denied herself the pleasure of shedding. I thought he'd dive into these salted pools and swim himself to penance. He didn't. For forty days and forty nights I mourned Jo and the parts of myself I felt slowly giving up on me.

My stay in Hades became permanent. It was as if I had let myself trip and fall into a spiritual slumber.

NANDI

When I first met her I didn't like her much, this Jo that everyone had been talking about. At first, she came across as one of those stuck-up people with their noses permanently lodged in the air. There was something in the way she carried herself that suggested that if she could, she would change the scent of the air in her world. That was until I took the trouble of getting to know her and found that above that high hanging nose of hers stood a browbeaten temple, perfectly disguised by a tender soul that life had forcibly hardened.

News of her passing stabbed me in the gut and formed a hernia in my soul. I think it was because I had once lived her life and transcended it, that I hoped she too would do the same. Perhaps if I had not had so much hope I could have done a bit more to help her see that her condition wasn't unique to her. Maybe I could have told her more of the story of my life: that I too had been kicked around, slapped around and bashed about. I could have possibly given up civility and my need for her to think me well-read, well-travelled and generally well. If I had been sincere enough, I could have shown her the lesions in my heart that I got from offering pearls on golden platters to swine content with only frolicking in mud.

Even though I knew Vido was the same calibre of brute as the ones I had encountered in my life's journey, there was something in him which I heard cry out for a shoulder to lean on. He had worn Jo's out, leaning on it longer than any one person should lean on another before the inevitable fray sets in.

Parts of me wanted to rush over and strangle him for taking away from me the one woman I had allowed myself to grow fond of in the longest time. Other parts wanted to light a candle and say a prayer for the living dead, for him. These urges battled it out inside me. None won. I did not do anything. How could I? Even if I had gone to speak to him, I suspect, because of the contempt with which I knew he held me, my words would have had a hard time making it out through my teeth. I would have felt odd saying the things I really wanted to say to him. I would have been self-conscious about my words in his disparaging presence, and felt them too big, too insincere, too contrived, two sizes too small to affect him in the ways I meant to. I dreaded his thinking me too contrived, too liberated, too gawky, too foreign, and too lesbo to have anything worthwhile to say to his gung-ho threadbare masculine ego. I kept quiet and took to speaking only in my heart, like Jo had been given to doing.

I knew very well how Vido felt about me. And it was not very well. In my presence, in his house or anywhere else I encountered him, he assumed one of his many personas and consistently manifested himself as the 'Minister of Homophobic and Misogynistic Affairs'. That's how I knew that whether it was the strangle or the prayer I gave him, neither would be received in a good way.

It's odd how we cripple ourselves with these thoughts.

For days I tried, without much such success to wriggle vignettes of wisdom from my books to pull me through this heart-wrenching time. I lay in a state of emotional paralysis. I gave in to inertia after my deliberate search for a koan or two to calm my mind and comfort myself. I let myself slip into an envelope of lethargy and found little sense in the words that once resonated, of 'whatever happens, we must continue to chop wood, fetch water'. I did not want to. I just wanted to sit there in Teddy's arms and do nothing but cry.

I was inconsolable. Strange how it was just three days ago that I thought I was ready to read Jo the one koan I thought would take our relationship to another level.

> The body is a Bodhi-tree
> The soul a shining mirror:
> Polish it with study
> Or dust will dull the image

I guess I waited too long. Hoping her mind would be polished by what I really wanted to say to her. I've always struggled with that. Instead, her skull was cracked open, her light dulled.

In the mirror of her eyes, now permanently shut, I felt my past life raise its head and make demands to be disinterred from out of the rotted casket I had buried it in eons ago.

A million and three spear-shaped splinters pierced my body. The only hands I would allow to touch me, to ease the throbs in my heart and contain my grief, were Teddy's. And so, into its bosom I pushed my face to extinguish my anguish. It soaked up my tears and made little fuss about their taste.

DIAPANTE

A scarlet moon rose the night before Jocasta died and I knew I was ready to receive the song she had been playing silently in her heart, for all whose ears were attuned to listening. Pity I was the only one, other than Anna, to have heard it.

Songs like that do best when collaborated on. I am afraid I could not match the tone of Anna's cries; they were pitched a note higher than my guitar would allow itself to be tuned.

I knew in the way her melody strummed my pain that I would have to make myself play it at Jo's wake, in or out of tune.

It would not have been the first time I played something off-key. Nothing lowered one's standards faster than years of busking for a street audience gagging to empty the jingles at the bottom of their handbags into upturned hats, if only to hear the clanking of their benefactor coins that tumbled out, interrupting my inebriated, discordant plunks.

But, no matter. Because I found that, for me, melodies played out of tune were the best ploy to detract people from their real pain. At least then they could focus on how annoying my appalling singing was and forget, even if for a second, the real reason for their anger.

On the night of Jocasta's wake I managed to play the ragtime blues ditty she had told me to sing, without missing a note. I even managed to master all the treacherous syncopated notes the best, as I had heard them streaming out of her tightly strung heart. A feat I accomplished even though I never really liked her much. Or Vido for that matter. There was something about her that reminded me too much of the life I had lived and was struggling to forget.

With the song accomplished, I set out to fix my larynx to let out, for the remainder of the night, the most discordant of notes to ease the heartache of those who were still sober enough to feel their hearts beating.

That evening, I was determined to say very little and just sing. I kept my shades on the whole night, even though the red moon did not let out a glare bright enough to hurt my eyes. I kept them on because I didn't want the truth stuck behind my eyes to shine through and embarrass me when I was least prepared for it.

Besides, I knew that most of the words that would be said tonight would drop from that out-of-tune-motor-mouth Pastor Paul's lips. And boy, did he spew out words from his ample mouth! He subjected us all to a soporific delivery of his remixed version of hellfire and damnation 'for women who refuse to', as he said, 'in line with our Lawd's teachings, learn in silence with all subjection.' I put a melody to his preaching to keep me from falling asleep.

'Let the women learn in silence with all subjection. But I suffer not a woman to teach, nor usurp authority over the man, but to be in silence!'

He went on like the hollow drum he was, complements of his namesake, brother Paul, in his first lyrical love letter to 'Tim the Man'. He was on a roll, you see, and was not about to stop.

I kept tapping my feet until my laces came undone. He was reaching crescendo!

'Beware the slanderer!'

'And the profane old wives!'

'The tattlers!'

'The busy bodies, speaking things they ought not'

'The gossip mongers!'

'The vain babblers!'

'The gibber-gabbers!'

'The whiny mamas!'

'The nag you till you can't do shit but kick them in the eye harlots!'

Dragging that line of thought, he managed to put to permanent sleep all the roaches, all the rodents and all the termites that Jo had failed to get rid of while she was still alive.

Even the three teetotalling sisters who were famous for their ability to turn any event into a lugubrious fanfare were seen intermittently fishing their heads out of the abyss of boredom he was determined to inter everyone in.

PAUL

Very little truth is told on occasions such as these. Even so, one can still pick up specks of it in the eyes of those who are not practiced liars. People with a penchant for black clothes have a way of hiding it best under the cover of all those layers.

My job is complex and constantly forces me to vacillate between instilling fear in people, as is demanded of someone of my vocation, and consoling them, a defect of my personality. When I started a frantic search for authentic words at Jocasta's wake but could not find any, I knew that it was to the spiritual manual I would revert.

Hellfire and eternal damnation were what I would give my grieving audience, even at the risk of boring them to death. I had hoped to put them to sleep in the first ten minutes of my speech so that I could just carry on saying whatever my own bored and tired mind could muster from that point on.

I cleared the frog in my throat – as is part of my performance – before I could say anything. Then I began my rehearsed, now rehashed to death script.

'Let the women learn in silence with all subjection, blah, blah, blah,' I said like I had said a million times before.

Beware the slanderer, the this that, the that this, the hoochie mama, and so on, and so forth. It worked. They sat uncomfortably, perfecting the famous pretend-I-am-awake-at-a-wake-posture. I could not be bothered.

Jocasta was at the back of my mind. I could not get over just how sly she was, that one. Going about with her bent Sunday head, pretending to be silent and submissive, when deep down, deep down she was as rebellious as that Nandi creature. Speaking in her heart as she always did. If she had been present in the Garden of Eden the story would have been different. She would have sold the apple back to the snake at a profit, she was so cunning.

Before they fell asleep, I always reminded my congregants that nothing good happens to people who disobey the Lawd's word. It should be simple enough for women to do as it says in the good book: you wives will submit to your husbands as you do to the Lawd. For a husband is the head of his wife as Christ is the head of his body, the church. A simple instruction on submission, written in crystal clear language, but does anyone listen? Bloody feminist-nyeminist heretic teachings brought by that stupid Nandi to the women's fellowship, leavening my fragile flock.

But for the things that happened in his house, Vido must be held responsible. His downfall was that he was a man of selective recollection. When I told him to take a little wine for his stomach and his infirmities, he remembered only the 'take wine' bit and did not only take it to cure his illnesses, but allowed it to be his downfall.

My spirit had been stirred countless times to tell Vido to leave that woman, Jocasta. But a man of my vocation knows better than to recommend the only action THE UNKOWN GOD was so forthright as to speak his hatred of – divorce. Even for those who suffer unspeakable feminine wiles.

When he called me and the only coherent things he said were the ones I picked up from the pauses in between his words, I knew that one of the vows he had made without thinking through had been fulfilled.

She had at last died and set him free. Very seldom does my heart go cold when one of my flock dies, but Jocasta was slowly becoming the yeast I was afraid would ferment my parish if left unchecked. Especially the women folk. She and Nandi had grown a bit too close for comfort. She had allowed herself to be possessed by that demon of feminism that drove women wild with the desire to speak their minds.

So, if I am to speak honestly – a privilege I seldom allow

myself – I received the news of her departure partly with a level of felicity and partly with the professional guilt expected of someone in my position.

I always knew that Vido would fail completely at developing Timothy's faith. He had no difficulty taking in the Acts of the Apostles but the book of Timothy was hardest for him to swallow.

That is why he allowed that insubordinate wife of his to speak back at him. Women's rights, he justified it. What women's rights when the word of God is so clear? There is no room in God's heaven for men who refuse to take a stand.

But it caught up with him, his disobedient spirit. And the pointiest point of his repressed anger did the trick!

He waited too long, if you ask me. Way too long. The word of the Lawd is straight and two beers on this issue, there are no in-betweens: wives, submit to your husbands, finish and klaar. The Lawd does not make room for women to bargain for a power sharing arrangement with their husbands. The good book does not say 'husbands, observe the equity bill in your household'. No, it does not. It does not even say be equal and happy together, no, none of that. It is simple and straightforward in its precept of submission.

Jocasta, if you ask me, got what was coming to her.

LEKGOTLA

A sombre cloud hung over this ghost-house-court-house, home of treaties, precedents, case law, customary law, enacted law, all manner of law, on the day I called everyone in to talk about Jocasta's predicament. The only law absent was that of love.

I felt very strongly that we could no longer afford losing women to shoes, or fists, or trysts, or kitchen counters; because of noodles, or squabbles or demotions or detonated tempers.

Stronger still, I felt we needed to exorcise ourselves of our demons, invite love back, and start all over again.

So I put it to all present, the two questions I thought would help us get to the bottom of Jo's plight. Vido, Ester, Delilah, Nandi, Diapante, Paul, Anna and Jocasta, too, whose body was not with us but whose soul I felt roaming with that cloud.

I asked them to search their hearts for the reason we had all been conspirators in Jo's death. I asked them, also, why we had all muted our voices and not expressed our intolerance of this happening.

I had my own ideas, no doubt, but I was not going to impose them on anyone. I thought it best if we all put our heads together and came up with the answers that would maybe help us take a joined first step to a different place.

From Jocasta, I wanted to find out why, knowing the things she knew, she allowed herself to be killed, like that no less.

I did not expect them to have answers and I was pleasantly surprised when they did. From the bottom of their souls, as I had asked them to prepare for this meeting.

They spoke of many things but mostly of breaking free from the ropes and chains that held them bound. If you were present you would have heard them speak like this.

VIDO

Sorrow permeates every single one of my memory cells. Every step I take follows its tracks; a counsel of forbears leads the way, egging me on. I know these things; I saw them even before I could see clearly. From the time I was an embryo my life was arranged to mimic that of a bull with no regard for china. This grave desire to smash into a one million and three shards all fragile things I encounter. The ones I don't insist on hardening, at least.

NANDI

My lot are a tribe of sages who came from a time before genesis. We lived in a garden which our foremothers filled only with apples. They encouraged us to eat as much as we wanted so we could know. I guess we relaxed in our knowledge, so we did not see genesis coming, nor did we see the chains He would insist we wear around our necks, choking us into silence.

DELILAH

I chose without thinking it through: a driftwood existence. I spend my days floating towards trenches of quicksand, dragged this way and that by waterfalls, following dead-end streams. Taunting my heart with hopes of home in a different pair of shoes, loving strangers with a fondness for broken hearts, praying that the layer of golden eggs would visit me. Now that she has, I spend my days cursing the bird with every negative vow I make. I sink into the chasm in my soul.

JOCASTA

First, he put a crown of rubies on my head, then he put a string of red popsicles in my heart. On both occasions I let him; I did not know differently. The same crown and the same string had sat on my mother's head and heart, like they had on her mother, and her mother's mother before her.

At first it did not seem strange what he did to me first with his palm. Then with his back hand, then with his fist, then with his head, then with his mouth, and finally, with his shoes. There was a part of my body that remembered it happening before.

My first bite of the red apple, a sage once told me, would have been my one way pass out of my genesis; I should have taken it while there was still time. I stood too long behind that shield of silence. Even though it offered me nothing, nothing and even more nothing in protection.

ESTER

Irresistible is the seduction of blood ties that bind. Under their spell blind spots appear where compassion should stand. The lure of ancestry mutes my voice. Mesmerised, my shadow constantly leaps to the fore, making choices that favour good manners above truth(s). My soul has sunk to the bottom of my translucent feet. Drained of blood, I can no longer walk.

PAUL

The sum of 'my' thoughts/feelings lives in a book bound in black. I have none that aren't written down, I can't say I ever did. Light dances at the back of my mind, I spend days ignoring the log in my own eye but do not tire of removing the specks in the eyes of my flock. I know it has not always been like this; it wasn't until I started pushing the book with the bleeding edges as the only truth. Now I use all my time covering up that lie.

DIAPANTE

When fists cause fits with irreversible effects, and booze gives numbing buzzes, and the birds and the bees peck and sting at each other, and jabs of pain are the only sensations we get from jam sessions, we know it's time to free ourselves from the hold of the tight strings that break every time they are strummed. And so, we should.

ANNA

I do not have much to say; one should not speak too much in the presence of grown-ups. I thought I should be quiet and swallow my words like I had learned from my mother, but she'll have none of it. She insists I share with everyone what she once told me were the colours of her life. Worse than speaking too much in the presence of grown-ups is refusing to take instructions, especially from those who live in worlds where bodies are not an accessory to life.

So, I speak her words on her behalf.

pink

the colour of the carnations
he gave me when we first met
that matched the colour of his gums

which showed every time he smiled
bringing up the joy that filled his heart

blue
the colour of his favourite shirt
that put him in a good mood
drew song from his heart
put a spring in his step
extracted delight from the depths of his soul

brown
the colour of the bottle
that turned his eyes red
propelled his anger
fuelled his rage
exacerbated his frustration

blue
the colour of my eyes met with his rage

the colour of the rest of me
his anger realised

pink
the colour of my dress, once white,
in blue waters
the day after his frustration
spilled onto me

blue
the colour of the sky from where I lie

the lights in the emergency room
the doctor's gown
my mood
my state of mind

                pink
the roses that now adorn my casket
my little girl's blanket in her cot, inconsolable

          blue
the insides of my casket
a white dove perched
on a mulberry tree
an olive leaf hanging from its beak

pink and blue
the colours of my life.

JOCASTA

They spoke these conspirators in bondage. And because they spoke sincerely, the cloud started lifting slowly. It lifted because they had spoken the truths that mostly go unspoken because no one ever asks of them to be.

JV Mdluli Estates

For a man who had worn a Garmin that had not registered anything less than 10 000 steps since the day he first strapped it around his wrist in 1994; a man who had managed to burn no less than 338 calories a day between the treadmill, aerobics and spinning; one who had maintained a 55 beats per minute at rest and a 175 beats per minute active heart rate for two years straight; a man who had kept a fastidious watch on what he ate (but not so much what he drank); a man who counted his calories and endeavoured at all times to strike a balance between his intake of carbohydrates, his fats – the unsaturated, monounsaturated and polyunsaturated – as well as his protein; the news of his high blood pressure came as a huge surprise to Jaco van Tonder. The kind of surprise an ardent Christian that had just caught a glimpse of the apocalypse on the evening news and was trying to make sense of it happening without them being privy to or being part of it, might experience. As the doctor's words reached his ears, his nose instantly turned a light shade of red. The sweat glands on his forehead opened and secreted a body of water meant to cool him down . The blood that normally flowed through his ears took a detour and in the twinkling of an eye his ears became as white as a sheet of paper.

It did not make sense. It flummoxed him. How could this

be happening? To him? At this time of his life? When, as they say, the best years of his life still lay ahead of him? What had he not done right? Was he not the pinnacle of fashion forwardness and health consciousness? Was he not the same man who had chosen to adopt a healthy lifestyle three years ago when his father, JanFourie van Tonder, had keeled over and died of a heart attack without warning, leaving him at the helm of an establishment he was not ready to command, but nonetheless, took in his stride? Was he not the same man who had managed to convince Laila, his wife of ten years, a woman who had been raised on nothing but koeksisters en melktert to abjure her sweet tooth and fall insanely in love with cucumber sandwiches? This is the man he was. This he knew as fact. And if this was the case, why then, did the universe and the science of medicine not know this? And if they knew, why had these two forces conspired to afflict him with a condition that he had done everything in his power to avoid?

The doctor spread something on his face which, to Jaco, looked like a cross between a smile and apathy. He kept his face in this state for the duration of his consultation, interrupting it only with a mismatch of twitches that did nothing to improve the initial look. During these interruptions he tapped his pen, which advertised a drug called sildenafil citrate on its side, on a notepad that had his name written in cursive script.

'To me, you seem like a man with good health, meneer. From what I am seeing you eat well, you exercise, you don't smoke. Given these results, the only thing I can think to be asking, meneer, is meneer stressed at home, or at work?'

Stressed at home or at work? Stressed at home or at work. Stressed at home or at work! Meneer held the doctor's words in his head and twirled them around as one might a single malt whiskey in a crystal glass.

First, he considered them as a question, then as a statement, and finally, as an epiphany.

Stressed at home, that he was not. Laila and the two munchkins had been nothing but paragons of perfection.

Stressed at work, now that was something else. Stressed at work, yes sir, that he was. The doctor had hit the nail on the head.

And the cause of this stress at work?

Parentheses.

Parentheses that had begun to appear in front of numbers on his Lotus 123 spreadsheet, where before there had been none. Parentheses spelling the demise of an empire that his father, die Groot Baas JanFourie before him, and now he, had spent years and years building out of the sweat of the brows of others.

And the cause of these parentheses? A man.

No, scratch that, that's not what he thought of him. The cause of these parentheses, that dom-stuk-kak-fokken-saat-sokkie-hoenderpoes-naaier he could not bring himself to call his brother-in-law. In other words, the cause was one Jabulani Vulamasango Mdluli. A good for nothing guttersnipe that his sister, Susan, had brought home and announced as her husband – now that this kind of thing could be done without transgressing any laws. For a woman who, on a clear day, possessed enough sense to make sound decisions, it baffled Jaco that his sister had seen fit to insult his entire family (those alive and dead) thus. By inflicting upon them this sorry excuse of a human being. Even more so because it did not seem as if this was one of those 'phases' that young white women of her generation were known to go through to make a statement, whatever that maybe have been. Nor did it seem like this was something she was doing to upend her mother's already topsy-turvy world. It seemed – and this is the part that concerned Jaco the most – that Susan really and genuinely loved this ragamuffin. Jaco, as he vehemently protested every time Susan suggested it, did not … how does one put it …? Dislike Jabulani just because he was black.

'Nee, Sussie, dit is nie waar nie,' he would flagitate, flaring his nostrils.

He would raise his finger in the air Groot Krokodil style, running the risk of raising his blood pressure even higher, and wipe the beads of sweat that would accumulate in the place where, if he had one, his moustache would have been.

'It is because he is dim sussie en daai is die waarheid. To me, he looks like the only thing he knows for sure is that if you spit on a pencil eraser it will erase ink. He's just dom,' Jaco would say the part about the pencil eraser with such smug conviction.

As if he, and not Dorothy Parker, had coined the expression.

Jaco was not the only person who took a disliking to Jabulani. The Board, which was really a fancy way of saying Mevrou van Tonder Senior (or Ounooi as Mildred would have it) also hated him. No, that is too light, detested him. But she, for a different reason. And that reason was the damage he had wrought on her company's bottom line. So strong was The Board's disdain for Jabulani – who for trading purposes took on the moniker JV Mdluli – that The Board could not bring itself to call him by his name, choosing rather to call him 'Onbeskofte Domgat'.

Onbeskofte Domgat was a tiny, puny, small man measuring no more than 15cms – I mean 1.54m. Jaco, who made it his business to know these things, knew his exact height. This, because once Jaco had tried, with very little success to convince JV – who, small as he was, was beginning to show signs of being pregnant with beer – to start exercising so that he could maintain a healthy BMI. For his size, and to invoke all mythology under the sun to explain the extent of this damage, JV could be said to be a man blessed with a far reaching reverse-Midas-touch. The caress of which was the cause of this 'stress at work' for Jaco. The effect of this reverse-Midas-touch was the reason JV lived in Jaco's psyche as the ambling irritant that ceaselessly plucked at his side, as if he were Prometheus' eagle.

The year in question was 1996. It had been three years since Onbeskofte Domgat had taken over the reins at Bokmakierie Estates. An establishment which, bending with the winds of change that were sweeping through the country at the time, had been renamed JV Mdluli Estates quicker than you could say hocus-pocus. At face value, yes, this was in line with the gust of changes that enveloped the country, but at the core, it was really Ounooi's strategy to attract more business from the government of the 'New South Africa Entsha'. JV Mdluli Estates, as it read on its advertising material was:

LOCATED ON THE LOWER SLOPES OF THE INIMITABLE AND BREATHTAKING TABLE MOUNTAIN, AND EXTREMELY WELL SITUATED FOR EASY ACCESS TO THE CAPE TOWN CITY CENTRE AND SURROUNDS. DATING BACK TO 1652, OUR LUXURIOUSLY

REFURBISHED ESTATE HAS SEEN A LOT OF HISTORY PASS THROUGH ITS DOORS. WITH ARCHITECTURE INSPIRED BY THE ARRIVAL OF OUR FOUNDING FATHERS – THE DUTCH, FRENCH AND ENGLISH – JV MDLULI ESTATES IS A SIGHT TO BEHOLD. WITH ITS ECLECTIC MIX OF STYLE, FUNCTIONALITY AND LUXURY, JV MDLULI ESTATES AFFORDS GUESTS A TRUE CAPE COLONIAL EXPERIENCE IN A RELAXED AND INFORMAL ATMOSPHERE. THERE IS NO BETTER PLACE TO FEEL AT HOME THAN HERE.

Thus described, Ounooi concluded that the estate would be in a position to attract a more varied patronage comprising the old and the young; the local and the foreign; the old-monied and the new-monied; the wheelers and the dealers; the hard at work parliamentarians and the parliamentarians only interested in catching up on lost sleep, and so on and so forth.

She couldn't have been more off the mark. Unbeknownst to her was the fact that her old clientele, that toffee-nosed brigade who were already nostalgic about a past they had hardly said goodbye to for two minutes, would find it impossible to lay their heads at an establishment known as JV Mdluli Estates. They wouldn't do it, they simply wouldn't. Not even if you paid them. This refusal despite the fact that a proper reading of JV Mdluli Estates' advertising material indicated that nothing much had changed in material terms, and that going forward nothing much ever would. But still, they refused to come, those wistful hoity-toity hard asses.

To be fair though, it was not only they who refused. The new target market, representatives of the New South Africa Entsha that Ounooi had hoped would come, also refused. But who could blame them? Because, quite frankly, what member of this new guavaman wanted to rest their heads, however weary, in any place where history had been passing through the doors, since 1652? Well, that's how they sold it in their advertising material; that's how they positioned it. And as the expression goes, 'that's the way the cookie crumbled'. Crumbling all the way into a multitude of parentheses before numbers, where there should have been no parentheses in Jaco's well-crafted Lotus 123 spreadsheets.

It had not occurred to the communications department (that is to say to Susan) that this light cosmetic change in the PR spiel would not hold any sway with the already weary but very newly elected cabinet of the New South Africa Entsha.

And so, began the change that Ounooi had not quite bargained on or planned for. And for three years she would have to sit and watch as JV's actions led to every bead of sweat evaporating from the brow of the drudge that had built JanFourie's empire for him.

It was once JV was at the helm of the Estates, and through no doing of his own it must be emphasised, that business began to take a nosedive. Where once before there had been throngs of people competing with history to pass through the doors of Bokmakierie Estates, there were now none. Where, once, the air conditioners had hummed their melodious song, cooling the air and making it crisper than a genetically modified lettuce that had been picked three weeks earlier, there was now dead, miff and stagnant air that had not moved in months. Where, once, there had been a minimum of three 'boys' – grounds men responsible for maintaining the manicured gardens, keeping the toilets free of any trace of shit or odour, keeping the grounds free of leaves and litter, the walls free of chips and cracks – there was now only an overworked and irregularly paid Mzwanele.

Mzwanele, JanFourie's favourite 'boy' from the time he was an actual boy. A time before he had gone and come back from ehlathini to find himself stuck in a limbo filled with personal nightmares that left him suspended somewhere between the state of being an actual boy and a man. A man who did not give much of a shit really, as long as he got paid.

Not that shit was not his forte. *Au contraire*, shit was very much his specialty. Mzwanele, you see, was a man who had seen an inordinate amount of shit after he returned from ehlathini. Any kind of shit you can imagine, he had seen it. Brown runny shit, brown solid shit, green runny shit, green solid shit left to float on the crapper, green solid shit on the hotel's bedding, splattered on walls by deranged nitwits, maroon shit with half-digested peas that suggested that the excreting party had a healthy dose of beetroot and some vegetables – good for them, not so much for Mzwanele – yellow shit, the kind one would expect only from newborn babies, brown-green shit, green-brown shit, thin shit, thick shit, slimy shit, bumpy shit, smooth shit: you name it, he had seen it. Not only had he seen it, he had spent most of his life since his time back scraping it off more surfaces than he cared to talk about. During his time ehlathini – a part of his life which he referred to as his 'former life' – Mzwanele had seen a different kind of shit. The kind of shit not discernible enough to the eye to be easily descibed, save to say that it was shit of great proportions. Life altering shit, if you like. Trauma causing shit, if you must. Shit that left indelible and irreversible scars on a person's psyche kind of shit, no doubt. And this is why everyone, except JV Mdluli, knew never to mess with Mzwanele.

Apart from the glory days of a trinity of 'boys', there had also been a time at Bokmakierie when there were at least ten chambermaids tripping over each other and dirty laundry, clearing out room service dishes and averting their eyes from all manner of bewildering things: a practice which they had learned without anyone having had to teach them. Burning the candle at both ends, and if that was not enough, the midnight oil too, 'Happy to be of service, merrem. Happy to be of service, sir'. And now there was only Mildred.

Mildred, Ounooi's 'girl' for twenty years, and now, in the new dispensation, her sister and part of the family. But only to the extent that no one thought it fit that she should be paid what she really deserved. Mildred, on whose shoulders it now fell to keep the hotel 'in tip-top condition' as Onbeskofte Domgat often said. A tall order which, in her incarnation as Ounooi's 'sister', Mildred did not take too seriously. So that slowly but surely, partly from neglect and partly from Mildred's disregard of anything that came out of Onbeskofte Domgat's mouth, the façade of the present began to wear off, along with the paint. And the bleak face of history began to reveal its ugly face from under the layers and layers of wallpaper that covered the crack that had been there all along.

It was palpable, this history, now that the hubbub had died down at the estate in ways that one could both sense and see.

In ways that you could sense, it was JV's office, where he spent an inordinate amount of time fixing his cravat, smoking his pipe and playing game after game of solitaire (a trinity of habits that irritated the bejesus out of Jaco). It was in the ghost of Jan van Riebeeck (1652), sitting stoically to the left of JV, squinting under his hat, not cracking so much as a Dutch smile but making his presence felt. It was on the miserable face of Francois Villion, later Viljoen (1671) right next to Ou Jan, wearing that infamous disagreeable French man's phizzog, incensed by the fact of having been ignored and later swallowed up by history. It was on the ghastly face of John Cecil Rhodes (1890), swathed in schadenfreude at Jabulani's failure, as if he had planned it himself. It was on the faces of the Khoi and San kings (unnamed and undated), peering through the windows from outside the house of history, having been denied space inside. It was on the faces of the Xhosa kings (also undated and unnamed), conspicuous by their absence. It was on the teary face of the ghost of Nonqawuse (1856), whose spirit had travelled a long way to stand there for her people, even if she, too, had to stand outside the house of history.

In the ways that you could see, this history was in the click-clack of memorabilia that ornamented Jabulani's office and in the cockroaches that appeared to be having a festive time crawling all over it. It was on the generic African masks favoured by amaphela. It was on the beer stein, the home of innumerable kakkerlak and their eggs yet to be released out of their oothecae. It was on the long opened and long drunk kitsch hand-painted bottles of champagne in which every cafard imaginable lived.

This is the corner of the hotel to which Mildred would direct Mzwanele every time he walked onto the estate, preceded as he always was by his standard question of, 'Iphi lembiba?' his way of enquiring into JV's where abouts.

Mzwanele called JV imbiba for two reasons: one, because even though they were last in vogue in 1985, JV continued to wear his double-breasted striped suits as if nary a second had passed. Two, because JV, especially in the presence of Jaco – and this only according to Mzwanele – always had a way of exuding the air of a field mouse.

'Iphi lembiba?' Mzwanele asked, in a voice as grave as the face he wore.

He had not heard about the parentheses, and even if he had, one could be certain that there would have been plenty little he would have known to do with them. The one thing he knew for certain, and this was his primary concern, was the fact that two months had gone by and there had still been no sign of a pay packet with his name on it.

He was hungry. He was tired. He was restless. But mostly, he was not amused.

'Iphi lembiba, and futhi, iphi imali yami?' he repeated, addressing no one in particular.

Mildred had heard about the parentheses in what her 'sister' had described as 'a recurring loss that might require further downsizing'. A loss, as her 'sister' had further stated, which had been caused by that Onbesokfte Domgat.

What was loss, when there were no people involved, but just numbers? Mildred wondered. What was downsizing when there were now only two people that worked at Bokmakierie? she mused. And the question that would not give her rest was, How was it that Jabulani had managed to singlehandedly cause a recurring loss of this magnitude, where her predecessors had failed at accomplishing such a feat?

Although these questions played themselves out in Mildred's mind, she had not acquired the language to ask them so she didn't raise them with anyone, only herself, and even then, only tentatively.

This lack of answers was the kind of shit that inflamed Mzwanele.

It was the kind of shit that drove him to the edges of a frenzy, enough for him to say to himself and anyone within ear shot, 'Hey, hey, hey man, ngath' izong'hlanyisa lembiba. Jessssus!'

Words which, even though they had come out of his own mouth, would surprise and frighten even himself in ways that they did whomever else had heard them.

'Lembimba must not drive me to go and unbury things that I don't want to unbury from the past.'

A sentence which was fine as it was, but as soon as it landed on Mildred's ears – who was now given to reading the thesaurus with the fervour that a newly converted Christian read the Bible – rearranged to, 'Lembiba must not drive me to disinter things from my past that I would much rather not.'

Either way, the effect remained the same. Sterner in Mzwanele's original words but, nonetheless, the same. The sameness of it further solidified by the fact that it was a threat, as real and live as it was, that only JV remained oblivious to.

The past that Mzwanele spoke of was in one sense, the real word as it related to the passage of time and the havoc that this had wreaked on him. In another sense, this past to which Mzwanele referred was a spot at the back of his RDP house (his only reward for all the sacrifices he had made) where he had, as Mildred would say, interred a little piece of himself.

'Umshini wami' as he called it. A part of himself that he brought with from his former life. A piece of machinery which, instead of handing over to the authorities in accord with the peace package of 1996, he chose rather to bury at the back of his house 'just in case the occasion ever called for it'. According to the representatives of the New South Africa Entsha and pundits of this package, its aim was to 'make peace compulsory and irreversible'. This idea, which was hopeful and forward looking, would later prove as most ideas that were being put forward at the time to have been the half-baked conception of a man who would come to wreak such havoc in the country's affairs in future, that it would bring the country to the brink of collapse. A man with a laugh so infectious it charmed hordes during the time of his rise and rise, and cloyed a multitude during the time of his fall and fall.

'Hey, hey, hey, ngizobulal' umuntu mina, madoda. Impshi stru, ngifunga uMa!' And just for emphasis, he also said it in English, 'Honest to God, me I'll kill a mutha, on my honour.'

Different nuance, same meaning. Either way, the fact remained that this was something he really meant and something he was perfectly capable of.

There was no one who offered a package to keep the peace in JV's head when Mzwanele almost walked in on Jaco, as they say, giving it to him.

'My father, and his father before him,' said Jaco with his arms akimbo, 'and his father's father before him, took more than two hundred years to build this business. And you, it takes you three years to un-build it.'

If Mildred had been around, she would have corrected that last bit to 'to destroy it'.

But she wasn't, so Jaco continued unchecked, 'What is it

with you people?'

'Us people?' Jabulani looked Jaco square in the eye, possibly for the first time in his life.

'I mean, what is it with you?' Jaco said, realising the breadth of the line he had just crossed. 'I gave you three years to prove yourself. In those three years, I did everything in my power to show you how things are done. And still … and still, after all of this time, by God, it amazes me that you would still not be able to tell what good business sense looked like even if it stood stark naked right in front of you, doing the break dance with neon lights sticking out of its every orifice!' Jaco screamed to the point of bursting his larynx.

He was no longer talking, so much as gesticulating. His mouth had long disengaged from his brain, so that there was no longer any link between what came out of his mouth and what he was thinking, if indeed he was still thinking. For his part, Jabulani clenched his teeth, suppressed every urge to sucker punch this imp, fixed his cravat, and asked for even more time, 'to do right by everyone'.

Concerning the veracity of Jaco's assertions of JV, the jury was still out on that. It was too early in the dawn of this newfound way of being between these two men – heck between everyone in the country for that matter – for Jaco to assume that he could make an assessment of the man's business savvy based only on three years of performance. When he, as he so correctly put it, through his people and his people before them, had more than 200 years of practice.

The morning after the night that Jaco received the financial statements from JV via his Hotmail account, they were unformatted, riddled with typos, grammatical errors and more parentheses than Jaco had ever seen in his life. He did what he did best; he took a strong drink and rid his precious spreadsheet of these errors. Every single one of them (except for the parentheses, of course, about which nothing could be done). Having fixed the document, he handed it to The Board, who correctly intuited that she would need a digestive to swallow the news that was being presented to her.

It was from vermouth, back then, that The Board sought solace. So, she fixed herself a martini – shaken, not stirred, an approximation of how she hoped she would feel after having read this document. Thirty minutes later, when that did not work, she fixed herself another – stirred not shaken, just in case this one did the trick. It did not.

To say that Ounooi was livid after she had seen those numbers would have been an understatement of grave proportions. Like her son at the doctor's rooms a couple of months before, her nose turned a light shade of red. The sweat on her forehead spewed down a chute and formed a small muddy puddle on account of the amount of makeup she had on. The blood that normally flowed through her ears took a detour and just as it had happened to her son before her, her ears turned as white as a sheet of paper. As a way of adding her own personal flair to these theatrics she gasped for air, her hands in that air, and let out a salvo of expletives to do with JV, that I do not think should be part of the telling of this story.

It would take a different kind of pluck for Mzwanele to eventually get his dues from the establishment that was JV Mdluli Estates. It came to him through a series of observations and a lesson he learnt inadvertently. Both the observations and the lesson came from watching Mildred who, because she no longer had any budget for Doom, spent whatever time she could spare between shooting the breeze with her 'sister' and playing Tetris, by killing what roaches she thought might present an affront to the establishment's theoretical guests.

All the while chanting, 'Silly.' Stomp-stomp, 'Silly.' Stomp-stomp, 'Silly cockroach. Silly.' Stomp-stomp.

Mzwanele surmised that if this scheme had worked for Mildred, then there was a good chance it might work for him too. So, he took a trip down memory lane and went to the past – by which I mean the spot at the back of his RDP house. With a steady and unhurried hand, he dug out of the hole remnants of the past as if he were digging out his umbilical cord to offer to his ancestors as sacrifice. He strapped these remnants across his left shoulder, very much like he had done in his former life.

With these remnants hanging on his left shoulder he walked to JV Mdluli Estates, through the gates, passed the ill-manicured lawns, up the stairs and through the newly refurbished revolving door through which history had passed over centuries, and into JV's office. Once inside JV's office he placed the past on the table, with Jaco present, and sensed a shift in the energy in the room, not only from those present, but also from the phantoms he knew shared office space with JV.

The fact that his past was not loaded was a little piece of information he thought best to keep to himself.

He put on his no-nonsense face, the same one he had last put on when he came back from ehlathini, and one that he found he had to avert his own eyes from when he sometimes encountered it in the mirror.

He spoke. Slowly. Deliberately. As if his every word were

a jewel that he did not want to lose.

He said, 'Hey gents, I'm not really in the business of killing cockroaches but if anyone does anything silly in here, and I don't get my money right here and right now, kuzawusimbakala.'

Jaco's Garmin issued an orchestra of sounds that suggested it might be malfunctioning.

Vulamasango, possibly for the first time since the new dispensation, spoke the truth in ways that would have made his ancestors proud and heard himself say, 'Hey bra, if you are going to shoot anyone in this room today, it is going to have to be this ngamla over here. Me, I'm just fronting.'

In that room, where History with a capital letter H, and history with a small letter h, brushed up against each other, it dawned on Jaco that from that point on he would have to start registering and monitoring a different kind of step. He had just experienced an insidious kind of stress, the kind that did not confine itself only to the workplace and for that there was no Garmin or doctor that could tell him what to do. For this kind of stress, it was going to be to the meaning of his own life that he would have to look.

ACKNOWLEDGEMENTS

This book would not have been possible had it not been for the generosity, gentleness and the love of all the people I am lucky enough to call family and friends.

I owe immense recognition to Makgathi Mokwena who, in the very early stages, had to suffer through incomprehensible verbiage that pretended to be writing. And in the middle stages, to Lwandile Sisilana; the first person to have ever read and given written feedback on any of it, officially making him my first reader.

The ears of Teboho Motebele, Apinda Mpako, Buyisiwe Putu, Mzwandile Nkutha, Tshegofatso Putu and now Rorisang Putu, would no doubt have bled a little less were it not for every second I proclaimed, 'I have an idea!'

I have been fortunate in my writing journey to have had access to some of the most generous minds and hearts, who have not only read my work with an acute eye, but have also given much needed and constructive feedback. I'm grateful to Makhosazana Xaba, who made it possible for me to join my first ever writing group. A group of women whose commitment to the word had us meeting on Saturday mornings to catch up on life and read each other's work. To Vossie Goosen, Hannelie de Klerk, and Yulinda Noortman, I will forever cherish those Saturday mornings and the space they provided for my fledgling voice. I'm also grateful, to Salimah Valiani, Shamim Meer, Shereen Mills and Frank Meintjies; members of my second writing group, who read as generously and as constructively over the greatest of wines and scrumptious meals.

I am thankful to my chosen family, with whom I spent a good three years of my life: the time it took to write most of these stories. Phumi Mtetwa, who opened her home and her wallet to keep me fed and comfortable. Maia Marie, who listened to the stories I was weaving but felt like the very first person in a while to take keen interest in the story of my life. Rayna, Davina, Mandy, Mamu, and Zen, for the wild times and the real times.

Gabi Ngcobo who said 'ubhale nawe,' when I felt the words leave me. Lewis Nkosi (my twin) who said 'the world waits, but it does not wait forever.' This one is for you Nkosi Yenkantolo. Bongani Madondo, who in his blues ways has been ever assuring and has more faith in my writing than I ever will.

My inherited rock star friends Siphokazi Magadla and Athambile Masola, who gave graciously of time they did not have to look over some of the stories. And for that, ngibamba ngazombini.

This book would have been drenched in waters flowing from rivers and rivulets, and would have been filled with repetition, had it not been for the thoroughness and accuracy of my editor, Katlego Tapala, who, in addition to listening to my woes (a service for which she was not paid), made me sound better than I could ever have imagined. I lack a million mouths to thank you.

Books come into the world because of people who believe in them. My unbounded gratitude goes to Colleen Higgs, who believed in this one enough to want to publish it. The point is not missed on me, that Modjaji is no ordinary imprint, but one that has the amplification of African women's voices at its core. I feel so blessed to have been invited to the table of those who have come before me, and those who will undoubtedly come after me.

Last and by no means least, my thanks go to the people who give my life sustenance and from whom most, if not all the stories I tell originate. To my mother, Thandile Nkutha, who can craft a funny tale out of any situation, in the shortest time possible and still keep a straight face. To my father, Mandla Nkutha, who can tell stories all day without tiring. To my elder brother, Mzwakhe Nkutha, possessor of the darkest sense of humour and my go-to person for remembering just about any funny moment. To my brother in law, Mpho Putu, whose heart is a bottomless well of kindness and love. And finally, to my partner in life and crime, Lerato Makate, who listens, reads, laughs, cries, cajoles, and often resorts to kicking butt just to get me to get things done (not just the writing). Thank you for bouncing back, and so rambunctiously at that, after the great scare you gave me when you got ill. My world would simply crumble without you, thank you for staying with me a little while longer, and thank you for putting me back together every time I break.

My eternal gratitude goes out to everyone who made this book possible. My not having mentioned you by name can be blamed on the shortcomings of my memory. Kunina nonke ngibonga ngiyachochoza.

Printed in the United States
by Baker & Taylor Publisher Services